John Hendricks Bechtel

Temperance Selections

John Hendricks Bechtel

Temperance Selections

ISBN/EAN: 9783337371609

Printed in Europe, USA, Canada, Australia, Japan

Cover: Foto ©Andreas Hilbeck / pixelio.de

More available books at **www.hansebooks.com**

Temperance Selections

COMPRISING

CHOICE READINGS AND RECITATIONS IN PROSE
AND VERSE FROM THE ABLEST SPEAKERS
AND WRITERS IN ENGLAND AND
AMERICA

Edited by

JOHN H. BECHTEL

Author of " Sunday School Selections," " Hand-book of Pronunciation,"
" Practical Synonyms," Etc.

Philadelphia
The Penn Publishing Company
1893

CONTENTS

Temperance Selections

FOR READINGS AND RECITATIONS

IT IS COMING.

D^O you hear an ominous muttering as of thunder
    gath'ring round?
Do you hear the nation tremble as an earthquake
    shakes the ground?
'Tis the waking of a people—'tis a mighty battle
    sound.

Do you see the grand uprising of the people in their
    might?
They are girding on their armor, they are arming
    for the fight,
They are going forth to battle for the triumph of
    the Right.

For the power of Rum hath bound us, and the power
    of Rum hath reigned,
Till baptismal robes of Liberty are tarnished, torn,
    and stained,
Till the struggling nation shudders as its forces lie
    enchained.

It has filled the scales of Justice with unhallowed,
    blood-stained gold,

And her sword to smite Crime's minions, now lies
  powerless in her hold ;
For the serpent of the still 'hath wrapt around it
  fold by fold.

It hath trampled o'er the hearthstone and hath left
  it desolate ;
It hath slain the wife and mother, it hath filled the
  world with hate ;
It hath wrecked the noblest manhood and hath
  laughed to scorn the great.

Shall it longer reign in triumph, longer wear its
  tyrant crown?
Shall it firmer draw its fetters, firmer bind the nation down?
Shall this grand young country longer bow and
  tremble 'neath its frown?

No! Let every heart re-echo; rouse, ye gallant men -
  and true!
Rouse, ye broken-hearted mothers! See, the night
  is almost through;
Rouse ye, every man and woman—God is calling
  now for you.

M. FLORENCE MOSHER.

HIGH LICENSE.

WE are at a point in reformatory movements in
this country where it is proposed to restrain or
control or stop the traffic of ardent spirits by com-

pelling the merchant thereof to pay a large sum, say $500 or $1,000, as a license. It is said that this will have a tendency to close up all the small drink-eries which curse our cities, and only a few men can afford to sell intoxicating drink. This money raised by a high license will help support the poor-houses, where there are widows and orphans sent there by the dissipations of husbands and fathers. Don't you see? This high tax will help support the pris-ons in which men are incarcerated for committing crimes while drunk. Don't you see? This high tax will help support the court of oyer and terminer whose judges, and attorneys, and constables, and juries, and police stations and court-rooms find their chief employment in the arraignment, trial, and condemnation of those who offend the law while in a state of insobriety. Don't you see? How any man or woman in favor of the great temperance reform can be so hoodwinked as not to understand that this high-license movement is the surrender of all the temperance reformation for which good men and women have been struggling for the last sixty years, is to me an amazement that eclipses everything.

My subject is, "High License, the Monopoly of Abomination." Do you not realize, as by mathe-matical demonstration, that the one result of this high-license movement, and the one result of the closing of all small establishments—if that were the result—and the opening of a few large establish-ments, will be to make rum-selling and rum-drink-ing highly respectable? These drinkeries in Brooklyn and New York are so disgusting that a man will not risk his reputation by going into them; and if a young man should be found coming out from one of those low establishments he would lose his place in the store. Now, suppose all these small establishments are closed up, and that then you open the palaces of inebriation down on the avenues. Here you will have a splendid liquor establishment. Masterpieces of painting on the wall. Cut glass on silver platter. Upholstery like a Turkish harem. Uniformed servants to open the door, uniformed servants to take your hat and cane. Adjoining rooms with luxuriant divan on which you can recline when taken mysteriously ill after too much champagne, cognac, or Old Otard. All the phantasmagoria, and bewitchment of art thrown around this Herod of massacre, this Moloch of consumed worshippers, this Juggernaut of crushed millions. It is not the rookeries of alcoholism that do the worst work; they are only the last stopping-places on the road to death. Where did that bloated, ulcerous, wheezing wretch that staggers out of a rum-hole get his habits started? At a glittering restaurant or bar-room of a first-class hotel, where it was fashionable to go. Ah! my friends, it seems to me the disposition is to stop these small establishments, which are only the rash on the skin of the body politic, and then to gather all the poison into a few great carbuncles which mean death. I say give us the rash rather than the carbuncles.

T. De Witt Talmage, D. D.

WHAT TO DRINK.

THE Lily drinks the sunlight,
　The Primrose drinks the dew,
The Cowslip sips the running brook,
　The Hyacinth heaven's blue.

The Peaches quaff the dawnlight,
　The Pears the autumn noon,
The Apple-blossoms drink the rain
　And the first warm air of June.

The Wind-flower and the Violet
　Draw in the April breeze,
And sun, and rain, and hurricane
　Are the tipple of the trees.

But not a bud or greenling,
　From the Hyssop on the wall
To the Cedars of Mount Lebanon,
　Is steeped in alcohol.

From all earth's emerald basin,
　From the blue sky's sapphire bowl,
No living thing of root or wing
　Partakes that deadly dole.

I'll quaff the Lily's nectar,
　I'll sip at the Cowslip's cup,
I'll drink the shower, the sun, the breeze,
　But never a poisoned drop.

GEO. S. BURLEIGH.

SOMETHING TO BE DONE.

THERE'S a battle to be fought,
　A victory to be gained ;
There's a country to be saved,
A host from sin reclaimed.

There's an enemy abroad,
　So subtle and so strong
That the conflict must be fierce,
　The struggle must be long.

We're recruiting for the ranks
　For years and years to come,
That our numbers may not fail
　Ere triumph shall be won.

MARY D. CHELLIS.

PUBLIC OPINION.

THE point of view from which I shall speak is that of total abstinence. It is, I know, the unpopular view, the depreciated view, the despised view. By taking it I rank myself among those of whom some speak as unpractical bigots and ignorant fanatics. But, because I believe it in the present need to be the only effective remedy for an otherwise hopeless evil, therefore I take it undeterred. Public opinion, my brethren, is a grand power. It is a mighty engine for good if we can array it

on our side. He who despises it must be either
more or less than man; he must be puffed up by a
conceit which mars his usefulness, or he must be
too abject to be reached by scorn. He, therefore,
that affects to despise public opinion stands self-
condemned; but yet public opinion has, many a
time, been arrayed on the side of wrong; and he
who is not afraid to brave it in defence of righteousness, he who, in a cause which he knows to be good,
but which his fellow-men do not yet understand, is
willing to be ranked among the idiots and fools, he
is a partaker with all those who, through faith and
patience, have inherited the promises. It was thus
—it was for the cause of scientific truth—that
Roger Bacon bore his long imprisonment, and
Galileo sat contented in his cell; it was thus—it
was for the cause of religious truth—that Luther
stood undaunted before kings; it was thus that, to
wake the base slumbers of a greedy age, Wesley and
Whitefield were content to "stand pilloried on
infamy's high stage, and bear the pelting scorn of
half an age;" it was thus that Wilberforce faced
in Parliament the sneers and rage of wealthy slave-
owners; it was thus, "in the teeth of clenched an-
tagonisms," that education was established, that
missions were founded, that the cause of religious
liberty was won. The persecuted object of to-day
is the saint and exemplar of to-morrow. St. John
enters the thronged streets of the capital of Asia as
a despised Galilean and an unnoticed exile; but,
when generations have passed away, it is still his

name which clings to its indistinguishable ruins.
St. Paul stands, in his ragged gabardine, too mean
for Gallio's supreme contempt; but to-day the
cathedral dedicated to his honor towers over the
vast imperial city where the name of Gallio is not
so much as heard. "Count we over the chosen
heroes of this earth," says a great orator, "and I
will show you the men who stood alone, while those
for whom they toiled and agonized poured on them
contumely and scorn. They were glorious icono-
clasts, sent out to break down the Dagons worshipped
by their fathers. The very martyrs of yesterday,
who were hooted at, whom the mob reviled and
expatriated;—to-day the children of the very generation who mobbed and reviled them, are gathering
up their scattered ashes to deposit them in the
golden urn of their nation's history !"

CANON FARRAR.

A MOMENTOUS QUESTION.

THERE is a question that comes down to all of us,
through the centuries, from the very birthplace
of mankind, full of momentous interest to every one
upon the footstool of God. It is that question
which Cain asked of the Almighty; not as a question, but as a defence against the arraignment of his
crime to his brother. It was, "Am I my brother's
keeper?"

In every civilized land throughout the globe, in

every civilized nation and state, and community, the answer comes back to that question, You are your brother's keeper. It is a responsibility that none of you can deny or evade. Every statute that you find in your statute-book for the punishment of crime and fraud is the question, "Am I my brother's keeper?" Every jail and prison that casts its gloomy shadows over the land, every sheriff and police officer, is the answer that the community makes to the question, as mankind itself; and besides this, and better than this, every reformatory and ameliatory institution that blesses this land, joins in the answer that we give to the question that comes to us almost from the Garden of Eden itself.

In the institutions of which we are so justly proud, where the mind is restored to those whose reason has been dethroned; in the asylum for the insane; in those institutions where the blind are almost made to see, the dumb to speak, and the deaf to hear; in every institution for the relief of the poor and distressed we have the answer of society to the question, "Am I my brother's keeper?"

In this great world of ours, springing as we all do from the hand of a common Creator, believing as we do in His fatherhood and the brotherhood of man, every one whom you meet on your pathway is your brother. He may be poor, he may be rich, he may be penniless, he may be humble ; but they are breth-ren of the same dust, pilgrims of the same family, travellers to the same tomb. If God has blessed you

with strength of will, that you have been enabled to
fortify yourselves, it is for you to lift him up from
that depth to which he has fallen, and put him
upon his feet, and to redeem him, if possible, from
a living death; worse even than the death of the
tomb.   It is the large-hearted, the social man, who
can not resist the temptation of the social glass; the
genial man, the generous man, whom the tempter
finds its victims.   It assails all classes alike; you can
find it crouching at the hearth-stones of the poor,
and it casts its gloomy shadow over the marble
mantels of the rich.

I tell you, my friends, there is only one way in
which you can resist the temptation.   There is only
one talisman, and that is: touch not, taste not,
handle not the unclean thing.

SCHUYLER COLFAX.

TRAFFIC IN ARDENT SPIRITS.

THE amount of suffering and mortality inseparable
from the commerce in ardent spirits renders it
an unlawful article of trade.

The wickedness is proverbial of those who in ancient days caused their children to pass through the
fire unto Moloch.   But how many thousands of
children are there in our land who endure daily
privations and sufferings which render life a burden,
and would have made the momentary pang of infant
sacrifice a blessing!   Theirs is a lingering, living

death. There never was a Moloch to whom were immolated yearly as many children as are immolated, or kept in a state of constant suffering, in this land of nominal Christianity. We have no drums and gongs to drown their cries, neither do we make convocations, and bring them all out for one mighty burning. The fires which consume them are slow fires, and they blaze balefully in every part of our land, throughout which the cries of injured children and orphans go up to Heaven. Could all these woes, the product of intemperance, be brought out into one place, and the monster who inflicts the sufferings be seen personified, the nation would be furious with indignation. Humanity, conscience, religion, all would conspire to stop a work of such malignity.

We are appalled and shocked at the accounts from the East, of widows burned upon the funeral-piles of their departed husbands. But what if those devotees of superstition, the Bramins, had discovered a mode of prolonging the lives of their victims for years amid the flames, and by these protracted burnings were accustomed to torture life away? We might almost rouse up a crusade to cross the deep, to stop by force such inhumanity. But alas! we should leave behind us, on our own shores, more wives in the fire than we should find of widows thus sacrificed in all the East; a fire, too, which, besides its action upon the body, tortures the soul by lost affections, and ruined hopes, and prospective wretchedness.

Every year thousands of families are robbed of fathers, brothers, husbands, friends. Every year widows and orphans are multiplied, and gray hairs are brought with sorrow to the grave. No disease makes such inroads upon families, blasts so many hopes, destroys so many lives, and causes so many mourners to go about the streets, because man goeth to his long home.

Can we lawfully amass property by a course of trade which fills the land with beggars, and widows, and orphans, and crimes,—which peoples the grave-yard with premature mortality, and the world of woe with the victims of despair?

Could all the forms of evil produced in the land by intemperance, come upon us in one horrid array, it would appall the nation, and put an end to the traffic in ardent spirits. If, in every dwelling built by blood, the stone from the wall should utter all the cries which the bloody traffic extorts, and the beam out of the timber should echo them back,— who would build such a house?—and who would dwell in it? What if in every part of the dwelling, from the cellar upward, through all the halls and chambers, babblings, and contentions, and voices, and groans, and shrieks, and wailings, were heard, day and night? What if the cold blood oozed out, and stood in drops upon the walls; and by preter-natural art all the ghastly skulls and bones of the victims destroyed by intemperance should stand upon the walls, in horrid sculpture within and with-out the building,—who would rear such a building?.

What if at eventide, and at midnight, the airy forms of men destroyed by intemperance were dimly seen haunting the distilleries and stores where they received their bane,—following the track of the ship engaged in commerce,—walking upon the waves,—flitting athwart the deck,—sitting upon the rigging,—and sending up from the hold within, and from the waves without, groans, and loud laments, and wailings? Who would attend such stores? Who would labor in such distilleries? Who would navigate such ships?

Oh! were the sky over our heads one great whispering-gallery, bringing down about us all the lamentation and woe which intemperance creates, and the firm earth one sonorous medium of sound, bringing up around us from beneath, the wailings of the lost, whom the commerce in ardent spirits had sent thither,—these tremendous realities, assailing our sense, would invigorate our conscience, and give decision to our purpose of reformation. But these evils are as real as if the stone did cry out of the wall, and the beam answered it,— as real as if, day and night, wailings were heard in every part of the dwelling, and blood and skeletons were seen upon every wall,—as real as if the ghostly forms of departed victims flitted about the ship as she passed o'er the billows, and showed themselves nightly about stores and distilleries, and with unearthly voices screamed in our ears their loud lament. They are as real as if the sky over our heads collected and brought down about us all the notes of sorrow in the land, and the firm earth should open a passage for the wailing of despair to come up from beneath.

LYMAN BEECHER.

A CRY FROM THE DEPTHS.

THE waters have gone over me. But out of the black depths, could I be heard, I would cry out to all those who have but set foot in the perilous flood. Could the youth, to whom the flavor of his first wine is delicious as the opening scenes of life, or the entering upon some newly-discovered paradise, look into my desolation, and be made to understand what a dreary thing it is when a man shall feel himself going down a precipice with open eyes and a passive will ; to see his destruction, and have no power to stop it, and yet to feel it all the way emanating from himself ; to perceive all goodness emptied out of him, and yet not to be able to forget a time when it was otherwise ; to bear about the piteous spectacle of his own self-ruin ; could he see my fevered eye, feverish with last night's drinking. and feverishly looking forward for this night's repetition of the folly ; could he feel the death, out of which I cry hourly with feebler outcry to be delivered, it were enough to make him dash the sparkling beverage to the earth in all the pride of its mantling temptation.

CHARLES LAMB.

A WARNING AGAINST WINE.

SOLOMON never said a truer word than what he says about those who tarry long at the wine. The questions asked by him, " Who hath woe? who hath sorrow? who hath contentions? who hath babbling? who hath wounds without cause? who hath redness of eyes? " are not only answered by Solomon himself, but we find his answers verified every day that we look into the news of the daily papers ; while around us, on every side, in the street, we may see living witnesses to the truth of what Solomon says.

Many whom I meet, who have become slaves to strong drink, say : " Oh, that I had never commenced to drink ; but now I have no power ; and drink is stronger than my own will ; stronger than my love for my wife and children ; stronger even than my wish for heaven."

May the dear children be kept from ever touching wine, or any drink that will intoxicate, so that they will be in no danger of the terrible consequences that follow those who " tarry long at the wine."

Remember, that those who are drunkards did not intend to become so ; they only thought of drinking just a little ; but the little kept increasing, and the love for drink kept growing stronger, until the eyes grew red, and the face grew bloated, and the step grew unsteady, until the one who might have been a blessing to the world and a help to those around him, has become a loathsome object and a terror to.

his friends.   It is not safe to take even a little strong drink ; because the love for it so soon becomes a strong and cruel master.

War is terrible, and many of our best men have gone to their graves through war ; but strong drink has carried more victims to the grave, in America, than has war.

Again, I beg of the young to touch not and taste not any strong drink.

D. L. MOODY.

STRIKE FOR PROHIBITION.

STRIKE for prohibition;
　Ask for nothing less;
Labor for its triumph,
　Pray for its success.

Put it in your school-books ;
　Teach it to the young;
Let it be the key-note
　Of the nation's song.

Sound it from the pulpit,
　Through the public press;
Speed it on its mission,
　Every home to bless.

With its holy incense
　Burden ev'ry breeze
From Lake Superior's waters
　To the Southern Seas.

Waft it on the zephyrs
Over ev'ry State,
From Atlantic's borders
To the Golden Gate.

Onward let the echoes
Roll from shore to shore,
Heralding the demon
Banished evermore!

TEMPERANCE.

MORE of good than we can tell,
More to buy with, more to sell;
More of comfort, less of care,
More to eat and more to wear;
Happier homes, with faces brighter,
All our burdens rendered lighter;
Conscience clean and minds much stronger,
Debts much shorter, purses longer;
Hopes that drive away all sorrow,
And something laid up for to-morrow.

PROHIBITION THE ULTIMATUM.

THE effects of alcohol are a crowning curse. Its horrors have never been fully portrayed. No pencil is black enough to paint the picture and do it full justice. No tongue is eloquent enough to tell the sad story in all its dreadful details. The

use of alcohol is a wide and withering scourge. It
is a physical curse, blearing the eyes, blistering
the tongue, deranging the stomach, paralyzing the
nerves, hardening the liver, poisoning the blood, co-
agulating the brain, inducing and aggravating many
diseases, and digging myriads of premature graves.
It is a financial curse, draining the pocket, inviting
poverty, diminishing comforts, multiplying miseries,
filling almshouses, and creating hard times. It is a
mental curse, clouding the judgment, dethroning
the reason, promoting ignorance, producing imbe-
cility, and transforming its unhappy victims into
maniacs and fools. It is a moral curse, weakening
the will, inflaming the passions, hushing the voice
of conscience, and preparing the way for every vice
and crime.

The attendant miseries of drunkenness swarm like
a locust plague. In the slimy trail of this alcoholic
serpent you find everything that is dark and dreadful—everything that is regretful and ruinous. You
find men without manhood, women without womanhood, age without solace, and infancy without hope.
You find want and woe, rags and wretchedness,
squalor and filth, disease and death. You find
broken vows, broken bones, broken fortunes, broken
hopes and broken hearts. You find bad manners
and bad morals; bad words and bad actions; bad
reputations and bad characters; bad plans and bad
performances; bad parents and bad children; a bad
beginning and a bad end. Surely, intemperance is
the crowning curse of American society.

The liquor-traffic is a gigantic crime. I bring against it the following indictments :

It is a destroying intruder. We need the store, the school, the mill, the church. These are all uplifting forces, and we bid them a hearty welcome. But where under the shining sun is there any need of a brewery, a distillery, or a dram-shop? What want does that supply? What sorrow does that alleviate? What home does that make happy? Does it add thrift to your farms, skill to your mechanism, brilliancy to your brains, or nobility to your character? There is absolutely no need of a single saloon in all our broad domain.

It is a fatal temptation and a snare. It is a man-trap and a death-trap. It multiplies its blandishments and lures its unwary victims to death and damnation. No wonder that Lord Chesterfield, in words as eloquent as they were burning, should say of rumsellers : "Let us crush out these artists in human slaughter, who have reconciled their countrymen to sickness and ruin, and spread over the pit-falls of debauchery such baits as men cannot resist."

It is a commercial fraud. It is full of shams, hollow pretenses, and false claims. It takes a blessing, and gives back a curse. It takes your money, but fails to return a fair equivalent. Bar-room bargains are essentially wanting in the principle of *quid pro quo*, or commercial honesty. Otherwise, saloonists would display their goods in their front windows, and put the drunkards they manufacture upon exhibition at the county fairs, instead of skulking behind painted panes and screened doors.

It is a monster of cruelty. It is conscienceless, unprincipled, and as cruel as the grave. It is a traffic in tears and groans and blood, in vice and crime and misery.

A. A. PHELPS.

ONE GLASS TOO MUCH.

"O HO! he has drunk one glass too much!"
  So I heard the jeering rabble say,
As a young man from the bar-room door,
  Goes reeling forth down the drunkard's way!
And I wonder as he staggers on,
  How many, many thousands such
The same dark road to ruin have gone,
  By drinking just "one glass too much."

A maiden sits at the banquet board,
  Her eyes aflame and her cheeks aflush;
Her lips have quaffed of the fiery draught
  That drives her pulse with a feverish gush.
Now she can laugh at the ribald jest;
  She shrinks not from the lecherous touch,
The sentinel sleeps in the maiden's breast,
  Alas! she has sipped "one glass too much."

A pilot stands at the quivering helm,
  While the waves with fierce and angry roar
Are drifting his bark through storm and dark
  To rocks that frown on a dangerous shore;

In vain do his nerveless, tremulous hands,
　　With 'wildered clasp the tiller-rope clutch,
A wreck on the rocks, a corpse on the sands,
　　That sailor has drunk " one glass too much."

A thousand patriots carry their flag
　　In the fight of freedom bold and high!
With lofty courage they're forcing back
　　The legions that strike at liberty;
And the shout of triumph almost peals—
　　The coveted prize they almost touch—
When ah! from his horse the captain reels;
　　And the day is lost by—"one glass too much."

" One glass too much! " aye, tell me, who can,
　　How long may the reckless tippler pass
The poisonous dram to his thirsty lips
　　And still escape from the fateful glass?
Young man, so strong in your generous pride;
　　Fair maiden, so blest with beauty's touch,
Oh, tamper not with the tempting tide!
　　The very first glass is " one glass too much."

AN EARNEST CRY.

GOD of the beautiful! God of the free,
　　Earnestly, hopefully turn we to Thee;
Turn we to Thee in this heart-stirring hour,
Seeking for strength in Thy goodness and power,
Asking our strength from the Wisdom above,
Praying for light from the essence of love.

Is not earth beautiful—is not earth bright,
Teeming with usefulness—beaming with light?
Hath not kind nature a harmony given—
Stamping on all things the impress of heaven?
Whence comes the sorrow, then—whence all this care?
What makes this wailing—this cry of despair?
Why all this discord—what makes the war?
Man is the guilty one—Man makes the jar.
Sold is his birthright, for passion, or pelf—
Lost to the brotherhood—lost to himself;
Conquered by appetite—blackened by sin—
Smothering the God-like that struggles within,
Joined heart and hand to the cold, selfish throng,
Cursing the earth with oppression and wrong,
Watching and waiting, like beasts for their prey,
Dealing out death to the young and the gay,
Blighting the buds of true love in the bloom,
Scattering o'er all things misfortune and gloom,
Crushing the heart of the mother with care,
Crushing the heart of the wife with despair,
Searing her love and destroying her trust,
Laying the hopes of her heart in the dust,
Beggaring her children, and making her life
Weary, and wayworn with sorrow and strife,
Binding in fetters the body and mind,
That Thou in Thy wisdom made free as the wind.

God of the beautiful!   God of the free,
Earnestly, hopefully turn we to Thee—
Give us Thine aid this dread curse to remove,
Give us Thine aid in our labor of love—

Guide us and guard us and lead us aright,
Let our lips utter truth, and our hands hold the light
That shall show to our brothers the death-bounded
    path
Their footsteps are treading in sorrow and wrath.

Wilt Thou not soften the cold hearts of steel,
Wilt Thou not teach men to love and to feel?
Show to our rulers the right from the wrong—
Show them the weak have a claim on the strong;
Bid them go forth to the contest of might,
Armed with the weapons of mercy and right,
To conquer the spoiler that stands by the way,
Clutching his victims by midnight, by day:
Bid them destroy from off our fair earth,
The demon of woe to the home and the earth;
Let them not faint till the work is all done,
And the shout goes to heaven of Victory won!

Lead Thou our people to see the right way,
(The night's darkest moments are just before day),
Give to our mothers the light from above,
Give to our wives the true spirit of love,
Give to our sisters the strength of the hour,
Give to our daughters persuasion and power,
Give them strong faith in the work they've begun,
Give them strong hope that the work will be done,
Patience and love till they reach the great goal,
And the waters of death cease to curse woman's soul.

Oh! may our efforts and words of good cheer
Usher the dawn of a glorious year;

A year of relief to the poor and distressed,
A year full of hope to the crushed and oppressed,
When the weak and the erring may walk without
　　strife,
Untempted, untried, through the journey of life,
And the victim redeemed from the rumseller's chain,
Shall stand in Thine image, unfettered, again.

MRS. F. D. GAGE.

OUR PLATFORM.

IF there is any one democratic principle known among men, it is the principle of the right of the people to abate a public nuisance, the right of the people to self-preservation. We claim, therefore, the right of the people in every community on all this continent to suppress, by legislation, the great nursery of crime, pauperism, degradation, immorality, and the destruction of what is, after all, the life-blood of the nation—its brain and its working power. The liquor traffic has not only drained the pockets and filled the almshouses, but it murders manhood; and, therefore, our American republicanism, as well as our Christianity, rises up in stern indignation, protesting against it, and demanding the right to suppress it wherever the people see fit to exercise that right.

Here are our principles: total abstinence, the reformation of men through the love-power, personal persuasion, and the right to suppress the tippling-houses by law. We welcome to our ranks all who hate drink, and drinking usages, and dram-shops; we widen our platform for all prohibitionists and moral-suasionists, asking them to stand side by side, shoulder to shoulder, and to work in the line God calls them. With God's help, henceforth there shall not be dissensions, bickerings, and alienations in the ranks of this great Christian reform. There is work enough for us all. We claim that no man can work with us efficiently who does not so hate drink that he is willing to put it out of his house and to put it out of his own hand. If he prefers to work in the line of prohibition, so let him work; or in the line of personal persuasion, so let him or her work. We have before us an ideal; we are striving toward it. People say of us teetotalers, "You are idealists." We are. This nation would not be what it is to-day but for the striving toward a glorious ideal that the Abraham Lincolns and the Charles Sumners kept ever before them as the mark of the prize of their high calling. The Christian Church is a company of idealists striving toward the stature of a perfect man in Christ Jesus. Just imagine a church drawing up a creed full of compromises! How long would that church live? Imagine a pulpit striving to preach a piebald morality! No, the temperance cause can not compromise. We can not sink below our ideal, which is as lofty as the Word of God and the welfare of humanity. We believe in touching not and tasting not intoxicating drinks. We believe in all efforts to suppress the dram-shop, and we shall still strive toward that end. The moment we lower the standard, the moment we compromise, the cause is gone, and we are gone with it.

I call upon you, therefore, to stand with us on the platform that to so many seems mere idealism. Paul was an idealist in the estimation of Athens, and Corinth, and Rome. If Paul had abated one jot, or compromised one line, where would the Gospel of Jesus Christ be? Let us put the mark as high as heaven. Let us take our tempted fellow-creatures by the hand, pointing them to that mark, bid them strive toward it, and ask God to help us to help them toward it. This is no hour for retreat. God summons this nation now, as He summoned it years ago, to enter the great conflict against the most terrible enemy of the nation's life and liberty.

"Deeper than thunder on summer's first shower,
  On the dome of the sky God is striking the hour;
  Shall we falter before what we've prayed for so long,
  When the wrong is so weak and the right is so strong?"
                                                    Rev. T. L. Cuyler.

THE DESTROYER.

INTEMPERANCE creates in man an ungovernable appetite. Men who have fallen have told us it is not a desire, not an appetite, not a passion. These ordinary words fail to express the thing. It is more like a raging storm that pervades the entire being; it is a madness that paralyzes the brain, it is a corrosion that gnaws the stomach, it is a storm-fire that courses through the veins; it transgresses every boundary, it fiercely casts aside every barrier, it regards no motive, it silences reason, it stifles conscience, it tramples upon prudence, it overleaps everything that you choose to put in its way, and eternal life and the claims of God are as feathers, which it blows out of its path.

What does it do to man's body? It diseases it; it crazes his brain, it blasts his nerves, it consumes his liver, it destroys his stomach, it inflames his heart, it sends a fiery flood of conflagration through all the tissues; it so saps the recuperative energies of man's body, that oftentimes a little scratch upon a drunkard's skin is a greater injury than a bayonet-thrust through and through the body of a temperate man. It not only does this, but the ruin that it brings into the nervous system often culminates in delirium tremens. Have you ever seen a man under its influence? Have you heard him mutter, and jabber, and leer, and rave like an idiot? Have you heard him moan, cry, shriek, curse and rave, as he tried to skulk under the bedclothes? Have you looked into his eyes, and seen the horrors of the damned there? Have you seen the scowl on his face, so that the whole atmosphere was filled with tempest? Have you seen him heave on his bed, as though his body was undulating upon the rolling waves like a fire? If you have, then you know what it does to the body.

It enthralls the will. A man's will ought to be king. The will of the drunkard is an abject slave.

The noblest and the mightiest men have been unable to break off the chain when it is once riveted. I verily believe there have been no such wails of despair out of hell itself as have gone up from the lips and heart of the drunkard who knew he never could be recovered.

What does it do to the heart? If a man is made in the image of God's intellect, a woman is made in the image of God's heart. A tender woman is tenderest to her child. Is there anything that can unmother a woman, that can pluck the maternal heart out of her, and put in its place something that is powerful and fiendish? Is there any other agent on earth, or even in the world of the damned, that can so transform a mother's heart into something for which thought itself can not find similitude? Satan himself can not do it; but rum can.

It wrecks character. It is a double shipwreck; the drunkard not only loses his own respect but he loses the respect of everybody else. His own character, with its real worthiness and with its reputation, is gone, and his worthiness in the estimation of other people is gone too—both of them, slain, are buried in one grave; and the grave-digger and the murderer, who are they? Rum. It wipes out the likeness of God from the soul, and makes a man a mixture of the brute and the demon, evolving the stupidity of the one and the philosophy of the other; and the Bible tells us that no drunkard shall ever inherit the kingdom of God.

REV. H. M. SCUDDER.

MY FIRST SPEECH.

YOU'D scarce expect one of my age
 To plead for temperance on the stage;
And should I chance to fall below
Portraying all the drunkard's woe,
Don't view me with a critic's eye, •
Nor pass my simple story by.

Large streams from little fountains flow;
Great sots from moderate drinkers grow;
And though I now am small and young,
No rum shall ever touch my tongue!

Now, where's the town, go far or near,
That sells the rum that we do here?
Or where's the boy but three feet high
That hates the traffic more than I?

THE TOAST.

POP! went the gay cork flying,
 Sparkled the gay champagne;
By the light of a day that was dying
 He filled up their goblets again.
"Let the last, best toast be 'Woman—
Woman, dear woman,'" said he:

" Empty your glass, my darling,
  When you drink to your sex with me."

But she caught his strong, brown fingers,
  And held him tight as in fear,
And through the gathering twilight
  Her voice fell on his ear:
" Nay, ere you drink, I implore you,
  By all that you hold divine,
Pledge a woman, in tear-drops
  Rather by far than in wine!

" By the woes of the drunkard's mother,
  By his children who beg for bread,
By the fate of her whose beloved one
  Looks on the wine when 'tis red,
By the kisses changed to curses,
  By the tears more bitter than brine,
By many a fond heart broken—
  Pledge no woman in wine.

" What has wine brought to woman?
  Nothing but tears and pain.
It has torn from her heart her lover,
  And proven her prayers in vain;
And her household goods, all scattered,
  Lie tangled up in vine.
Oh! I prithee, pledge no woman
  In the curse of so many—wine! "

MARY KYLE DALLAS.

AN ARRAIGNMENT OF THE RUM TRAFFIC.

WHENCE comes this spectacle in Christian lands? How has this alien grown up about our Christian altars to such dreadful proportions? It is here, and confronts us everywhere. It is the cancer on the face of Christendom, the blistering shame on the fair countenance of Christian civilization, engendered of the rum-shop, and the lust god of Mammon and pleasure.

The vicious classes are Christian born. Think for a moment, that this Christendom has authorized by law and sanction of the State, the creation of this frightful pest gang: that it has provided for its creation; that it is here not in opposition to, but of her will; that by formal and deliberate legislation, brought about by Christian votes, she has opened, in all her towns and cities, slaughter-houses of men, women and children, and of all virtue, and employs a million minions to do this dreadful work; that she has done this and continues to do it with her eyes open, and with full knowledge and purpose; that she has prepared and planned and deliberated in Government chambers for the production of these desperate classes; that her employed and licensed minions do this for pay.

For a generation Christendom has been hearing a low growl from the kennel, where she is battening these wild beasts of passion; a growl in the kennel as they have crushed their victims. "What means the roar to-day along Trafalgar Square and London streets?" It is the beast, loose and shaking his mane. Pamper him a little more on Government joints, and no kennel-bars will hold him. Fitted for raven, he will raven to the full. Rum engenders poverty; poverty and rum engender crime. From the Government rum-shop the wild beast hunts his prey. Is Christendom struck with judicial blindness, that she sleeps? Are her eyes holden that she cannot see? There are armies marching and countermarching, with banners on which are emblazoned dynamite, anarchism, communism, nihilism, labor-league, no-Sabbath, down with the Church and State, recruited from the dram-shop and officered from the kennel. Are we so deaf that we do not hear the tramp of the gathering legions? Nations that license murder for pay will be murdered for plunder; nations that batten the wild beast of passion will be devoured by the wild beasts of rapine and ruin. The rum-hole must be closed or the rum-hell will engulf Christendom. What shall be done with Christian rum, is the problem. What shall become of the Christian world? Answer it with license; or authorization, or tempering policies, it is difficult? Strike it down, cage the beasts that vend the frenzy in the only place to which they belong, the criminal cell, and the kennel will disperse. There is but one remedy. We have had experience enough to have learned what this is. The Nation must put an end to transforming men into beasts by law, and must put the beasts who do it into a limbo where their sorceries will cease. The conflict is now upon us. It is a life-and-death struggle. The Government is on the side of the beasts; the people make the Government. Shall the rum fiend still carry on his carnival of death? Shall the rum minions, at the still, behind the bar, at the bar, in the gutter, or in the mansion, rule? Or is there enough of manhood among us to save Christendom from the damning shame? The answer we make to that question determines fate. If Christianity has not power to save Christendom, where is our hope? With what face, then, can we go to the heathen? There is no devil worship in Africa more degraded, more lost to all sense of shame than the demon worshipper of rum; no high priest of the sorceries of heathenism more diabolized than the minions of Christian States authorized to manufacture and vend the poison. Paganism can muster no miscreants from all her realms more debased than the rum army; no festering pest-house—not even the Chinese opium den—more deadly to virtue than the Christian rum-hole. Must it be endured longer? Must the race be doomed to go into the future with this millstone fastened about its neck by legislators of Christian States? Are our tyrants too much for us? Then farewell to hope.

Who doubts that there is a remedy for this state of things? It is not unknown. This evil is rampant not of necessity, but we have not the courage or desire to apply the remedy. It is simply needed that right-minded people combine to do the work;

and in this, as in every case of a crying evil, the Church must lead in the reform. This is her most peculiar province. It comes in the line of the great class of moral issues of which she is the recognized guardian.

It cannot be effected by moral suasion, by sermons, by prayers, or by abstinence of the well-disposed. It is a case where the arm of the law, and force repressive, is the only resort. It belongs to the department of crimes; and must, of necessity, be met by criminal law faithfully executed.

BISHOP R. S. FOSTER.

SAMPLE ROOMS.

SAMPLES of wine, and samples of beer,
   Samples of all kinds of liquor sold here;
Samples of whiskey, samples of gin,
Samples of all kinds of bitters. Step in.
Samples of ale, and porter, and brandy;
Samples as large as you please, and quite handy;
Our samples are pure, and also you'll find
Our customers always genteel and refined;
For gentlemen know when they've taken enough,
And never partake of the common stuff.
   Besides these samples within, you know,
There are samples without of what they can do;

Samples of headache, samples of gout;
Samples of coats with the elbows out,
Samples of boots without heels or toes;
Samples of men with a broken nose,
Samples of men in the gutter lying,
Samples of men with delirium dying,
Samples of men carousing and swearing,
Samples of men all evil daring;
Samples of lonely, tired men,
Who long in vain for their freedom again;
Samples of old men worn in the strife,
Samples of young men tired of life;
Samples of ruined hopes and lives,
Samples of desolate homes and wives;
Samples of aching hearts grown cold
With anguish and misery untold;
Samples of noble youth in disgrace,
Who meet you with averted face;
Samples of hungry little ones,
Starving to death in their dreary homes.
In fact, there is scarcely a woe on earth
But these "samples" have nurtured or given birth !
   Oh! all ye helpers to sorrow and crime,
Who deal out death for a single dime,
Know ye that the Lord, though He may delay,
Has in reserve for the last great day
The terrible "woe," of whose solemn weight
No mortal can know till the pearly gate
Is closed, and all with one accord
Acknowledge the justice of their reward.

TWO REVOLUTIONS.

A LTHOUGH the temperance cause has been in
progress many years, it is apparent to all that it
is just now being crowned with a degree of success
hitherto unparalleled.

The list of friends is daily swelled by the addition of fifties, of hundreds, and of thousands. The
cause itself seems suddenly transformed from a cold,
abstract theory, to a living, breathing, active, and
powerful chieftain, going forth 'conquering and to
conquer.' The citadels of his great adversary are
daily being stormed and dismantled; his temples
and his altars, where the rites of his idolatrous worship have long been performed, and where human
sacrifice has long been wont to be made, are daily
desecrated and deserted. What one of us but can
call to mind some relative, more promising in youth
than all his fellows, who has fallen a sacrifice to his
rapacity? He ever seems to have gone forth like the
Egyptian angel of death, commissioned to slay, if
not the first, the fairest born of every family. Shall
he now be arrested in his desolating career? In
that arrest, all can give aid that will; and who shall
be excused that can and will not? Far around as
human breath has ever blown, he keeps our fathers,
our brothers, our sons, and our friends prostrate in
the chains of moral death. To all the living,
everywhere, we cry, 'Come, sound the moral trump,
that they may rise and stand up an exceeding great

army;' 'Come from the four winds, O breath! and breathe upon these slain that they may live.' If the relative grandeur of revolutions shall be estimated by the great amount of human misery they alleviate, and the small amount they inflict, then, indeed, will this be the grandest the world shall ever have seen.

Of our political revolution of '76 we are justly proud. It has given us a degree of political freedom far exceeding that of any other nation of the earth. In it the world has found a solution of the long-mooted problem as to the capability of man to govern himself. In it was the germ which has vegetated, and still is to grow and expand into the universal liberty of mankind.

But with all these glorious results, past, present, and to come, it has its evils too. It breathed forth famine, swam in blood, and rode in fire; and long, long after, the orphans' cry and the widows' wail continued to break the sad silence that ensued. These were the price, the inevitable price, paid for the blessings it brought.

Turn now to the temperance revolution. In it we shall find a stronger bondage broken, a viler slavery manumitted, a greater tyrant deposed; in it, more of want supplied, more disease healed, more sorrow assuaged. By it, no orphans starving, no widows weeping; by it, none wounded in feeling, none injured in interest, even the dram-maker and dram-seller will have glided into other occupations so gradually as never to have felt the change, and will stand ready to join all others in the universal song of gladness. And what a noble ally this to the cause of political freedom? With such an aid, its march cannot fail to be on and on, till every son of earth shall drink in rich fruition the sorrow-quenching draughts of perfect liberty. Happy day, when all appetites controlled, all passion subdued, all matter subjected; mind, all-conquering mind, shall live and move the monarch of the world! Glorious consummation! Hail, fall of fury! Reign of reason, all hail!

And when the victory shall be complete—when there shall be neither a slave nor a drunkard on the earth—how proud the title of that land which may truly claim to be the birthplace and the cradle of both those revolutions that shall have ended in that victory! How nobly distinguished that people who shall have planted and nurtured to maturity both the political and moral freedom of their species!

ABRAHAM LINCOLN.

A WORD TO YOUNG MEN.

I WANT to say a word to the young men. It is a grand thing to be a young man; to have life before you. Life is behind me. My record is pretty nearly made; yours is to make. I can't change my record to save my life. I can't undo a deed I have done or unsay a word I have spoken to save my soul. No more can you. You are making your record. We old men have our record nearly made, and we can't change it. It is an awful thing when a man is sixty-five years of age to look out upon a stained, smeared, smudged record, and know he can't change it. Thank God, there is a man who can wipe out the iniquity sufficient to save us, as a school-boy wipes his sum off the slate. Even if a man is forgiven, it leaves a mark upon him he will never recover from—never.

Young men, you have life before you, and you will have to map out which direction you will take. They tell us that eight miles above us nothing animal can exist. It is death to all animal life eight miles in that direction. It don't depend on the distance you travel, but on the direction; and when a man takes a wrong direction he knows it. Young men, you need not tell me when you are doing wrong you don't know it. You do. There is not a young man that is breaking his mother's heart by dissipation, but knows it; knows that every glass he drinks will be a thorn in the way for him. He knows it. What do men say? "Oh! young men will be young men." They ought to be. I always look with suspicion on old heads on young shoulders. You young men can be young as long as you live. Years don't make a man old. There is many a man forty years of age who is younger and fresher at heart than some young old men of twenty-five who have broken themselves all down by dissipation. William E. Dodge never was old. He was young at seventy-eight, and entered into perennial eternal youth without ever knowing what old age was. So can you.

I thought it was a terrible thing to be old. The first time I ever heard myself called old, it was in a railway station. I was looking after baggage, and one of these baggage smashers said: "Old man, what are you looking after?" It sounded queer. I don't mind it now. I don't like it when they say: "Let us pray for our aged friend." I don't like that. That is a little too much of a good thing. There are always some people throwing things at the things you are fond of. A woman got angry at her husband and threw a squash-pie right into a picture, "God Bless Our Home"; and it was the best picture she had.

I would say, then, to young men, there is no power, in my opinion, to-day to be so dreaded by us as a nation, as individuals, as communities, as this evil of drink, and it rests with young men to fight it.

JOHN B. GOUGH.

TOUCH IT NOT.

SANCTIONED by custom, licensed by the State,
　Worshipped by rich and poor, by small and great;
Sung of by poets, praised by doctors, too,
Caressed alike by pulpit and by pew;
The demon Drink reigns proudly o'er the land,
And few indeed his cunning wiles withstand.

The yellow barley bends to the light breeze,
And grapes in clusters load the trembling trees.
God's precious gifts for man to love and use,
And not to wildly squander and abuse!
If from a king the mandate should go forth,
From east to west, from sunny south to north,
That all the barley waving in the field,
And all the grapes the well-kept vineyards yield,
Should in the ocean recklessly be thrown,
There would arise one universal groan,
And men would execrate the tyrant's name,
And pile his memory with undying shame.
But man, a tyrant to himself, does worse:
Turns a rich blessing to a frightful curse!
Crushes the grapes and barley till the life
Once filled with comfort is with ruin rife;
God made the barley, but man made the beer;
A truth which to the youngest child is clear.
But some who love their drop, make this excuse—
"God sent these blessings for our moderate use!"
But what is moderation? tell me, pray!
I know some hopeless drunkards who still say
That they are temperate men; how can that be,
When all the world their drunkenness can see?
Where do the drunkards come from? Do you know
They from the ranks of moderate drinkers flow.
But do you say, "I never take too much"?
Pardon me, friend, I have known many such.
Proud of their firmness, they have stood awhile,
And met all cautions with a pitying smile;
But habit, though a chain of flowers at first,

Has grown a burning band they could not burst;
And with the drunkards they must take their place,
And share their awful misery and disgrace.
We strive from our fair land to wipe this blot,
And lift on high the warning—"Touch it not!"
First, for your own sake, throw the drink aside,
Let Temperance be your helpmate and your guide;
Next, for the sake of weaker ones, abstain,
And strive to win the drunkard back again.
Oh, for His sake, who came to save the lost,
"Rescue the perishing" at whatever cost,
And lift your voice in palace or in cot,
A voice of warning, crying—"Touch it not!"

W. A. EATON.

THE BOYS WE WANT.

BOYS, we want you—Our Country wants
    True-hearted, noble boys,
To make your world a happier place,
    To purify its joys;
To stand among the leaders
    Of every righteous cause,
To spread o'er all the nation
    Right, just and blessèd laws.

Boys, we want you—Patriots call
    You to the conflict now;
Beneath the yoke of fashion's power
    See millions daily bow.

There are hearts with grief o'erflowing;
  Let us cheer them, if we can.
Come and help to burst the fetters
  Which surround your fellow-man.

Boys, we want you—Temperance wants
  Firm, consistent lives to-day;
Victory marks her glorious progress,
  Homes are bright beneath her sway.
Shall the drunkard, lost for ever
  In despair and anguish, die?
Let us take the pledge to save him—
  All together—you and I.

Boys, we want you—Jesus wants
  Your hearts His truth to spread;
Follow Him in storm and sunshine,
  Ever in His footsteps tread.
There's a world of light and beauty;
  This is not the traveller's home:
We are pressing on to Zion,
  And we want you all to come.

Boys, we want you—Glory wants
  Every one her crown to wear;
Each soul we've happier made on earth
  Will increase its lustre there.
Time is flying, dashing onward;
  Soon our day's work must be done;
And an earnest, prayerful life, boys,
  Is eternity begun.

A. SARGENT.

THE RUM EVIL.

IN the midnight calm and holy, when the world
    has sunk to rest,
When the spotless dew is trembling on the lily's
    folded crest,
When the sighing of the zephyr creeps and steals
    upon the ear
Soft and gentle as an echo wafted from another
    sphere,
I will leave my heated room, leave the darkness and
    the gloom,
  I will leave the crowded city, quit the crime-
    polluted street;
Wander through the meadows, where I may breathe
    a purer air,
  Feel a purer, holier, better earth beneath my
    straying feet.

On through silent lanes where rustling trees are
    nodding overhead,
Whispering tales to one another of the pleasant
    summers fled;
On through fields where corn is waving, as if in a
    sleep is heard
Some soft anthem stealing round it to whose melody
    is stirred;
Stars are glistening in the sky, dew-drops glitter in
    reply,
  Silent converse with each other violets and daisies
    keep;

Robin with the scarlet breast dreams of mischief in
   his nest,
  Flow'rets, tired of being happy, close their petals
    now to sleep.

Yonder is a cot half hidden in a robe of red and
   green,
Covered o'er with countless roses bathing in the pale
   moon's sheen;
Surely nothing less than angels dwell within that
   cottage there;
Winning fairies must be hiding round a spot so
   bright and fair.
To the window I will creep, through the lattice I
   will peep—
  Alas! that such an Eden should have such a hell
    within;
See the drunken father lie with his children weep-
   ing by,
  And a bower of beauty blackened with the awful
    brand of sin.

Out again upon the highway, all my heart with
   sickness numb,
From that cottage quickly flying to a village now I
   come;
Rows of cottages, surrounded by green fields like
   verdant seas,
Or like hidden treasures crouching in the shadow of
   the trees.
But as I am drawing near, frightful noises greet my
   ear—

Curses like the yells of devils, oaths that taint the
　　very air.
Never city built by man since the world its course
　　began
　　Could eclipse the scenes of horror that within
　　that village were.

"Rum again," I faintly mutter, as my footsteps
　　hurry by,
On past sights of drink and riot, evil plague-spots
　　to the eye;
Out again into the meadows, here at least I may
　　breathe free,
In this solitude of nature no drink traces shall I see.
Rivers glisten calm and bright in the moonbeam's
　　spectral light,
　　Laughing streamlets, never sleeping, leap down
　　the green hillside;
Now the nightingale's sweet song breaks upon a
　　list'ning throng
　　Of primroses and fox-gloves that beneath the
　　hedges hide.

But the magic note is broken by a shriek so loud and
　　shrill
That the streamlets seem to stagger in their racing
　　down the hill;
And I heard rude, clamorous voices, yonder by the
　　river's brink,
Grewsome curse and ribald laughter—can I never
　　leave the drink?

Back again into the town, with a spirit broken
down,
By the crime that ever meets me wheresoever I
may roam.
Vainly may I strive to flee, still the serpeut's trail I
see
Blasting, ruining, destroying every spot 'neath
Heaven's broad dome.

IRISH WORLD.

THE SPARROW MUST GO.

JUST think of it! The Mayor and Council, with
all the policemen of New Haven headed by the
State authorities, moving in one grand procession,
carrying banners inscribed, "The English Sparrow
Must Go!" And then, when all other efforts have
failed, imagine the editor of the *Palladium* at the
head of the Connecticut State Militia, leading a
bloody charge, at double-quick, against a flock of
English sparrows, and at each bound crying out in
thunder tones, "The English sparrow must go!"
Why this bitterness against the sparrows? They
never destroyed our homes. They didn't "set the
cause of Prohibition back twenty years." Nor have
they interfered with the colored man's right to vote,
stuffed a ballot-box or bulldozed any human being.
They have not corrupted our politics, robbed the
Nation of its manhood or a mother of her boy.
Then what is the trouble? Why, the English sparrow don't vote, consequently he is like the Chinaman

—got but few friends. If they only had "infloonce," every sparrow family would be furnished with a brass-wire cage. But what evil hath this little sparrow brought upon our country? We turn to the columns of the *Palladium* for this terse reply :

"Only a few years ago, the trees on the green were full of merry singing birds, that filled the air with their sweet songs and presented a picture of joyous happiness, as they flitted from branch to branch, or swooped down in the green grass in search of a worm. To-day not one of those birds can be found (nor worms either). They have been driven out by the sparrows." Just think of it—a naughty, naughty sparrow robbing an honest, upright jaybird of his morning worm ! No wonder that there should be a demand made that the combined powers of both city and State authority should be promptly used for the overthrow and immediate suppression of the authors of such an infamous outrage. "The English sparrow must go ! "

"Only a few years ago," there was a home in New Haven. In that home was a happy, bright-eyed intelligent, rosy-cheeked Christian wife and mother, in the prime of her womanhood, full of hope for the future. Her husband was a manly man ; affectionate, generous, noble and true. In our country's darkest hour, when it needed men, he bravely marched for the front under the old flag, offering himself as a sacrifice, in defense of the life of this nation. In that home were innocent children, who "filled the air with their sweet songs, and presented a picture of joyous happiness," which can never be forgotten.

That husband and father to-day is a drunken, bloated, miserable, mental, moral, and physical wreck, down in the gutter, penniless and friendless.

The rose has left the cheek of that poor wife and mother, her eyes are sunken and blinded with tears; no longer does she occupy that once happy home; the joyous songs of her once happy darlings are heard no more. To-day, in a remote tenement, she is found with her little ones thinly clad, hungry, and penniless; and as the winter storms drift through the open walls they hover over the embers of a fire that is almost gone. No longer do they greet papa at the gate with a smile and a kiss. With every ray of earthly hope gone, the dark clouds of despair settle thick around them. Oh, with what submissive faith that heart-broken mother turns unto God and says, "Thy kingdom come, Thy will be done."

It was not the English sparrow that destroyed this home. But it was our Government's legalized, law-protected, fattened, and perpetuated hell-born liquor vulture. When we come to the judgment bar of God, the man who stood at the saloon counter and dealt out the liquor that destroyed that home will be no more guilty than the man who stood at the ballot-box and gave sanction thereto by his vote.

Then let the fiat go forth, that by the grace of God, and the will of American freemen, this nationalized, home-destroying liquor vulture must go.

JOHN P. ST. JOHN.

THE DEATH OF THE REVELLER.

THE lights were gleaming and the feast was spread,
 And at the table sat the boisterous guests,
Shouting and singing snatches of coarse songs.
The giver of the feast was an old man,
Grown old in sin, and hardened more and more,
Till age found him, 'mid the boisterous crew,
A guide and prompter into any path
That led away from virtue or from truth.
His snow-white hair upon his shoulders fell
In twining ringlets ; and his silver beard,
Grizzled with age, clung to his hollow cheeks ;
And on his brow the plough of time had made
Deep furrows ; and his eyes were growing dim.
But still his hollow voice rang on the night,
And his eye glistened at the obscene jests
Of his companions, and his skinny hands
Beat on each other with a hollow sound
At the rude singing of the rabble crew.
It was an awful sight to see him there,
So old and withered, yet so wildly gay ;
So like a patriarch yet so like a fiend.
The ruddy wine was poured incessantly;
And as the brimming goblets passed along,
The old man chuckled, and his eyes grew bright.
He seized a flagon in his trembling hands,
And held it to his lips, and shrieked aloud,
The while it ran like blood upon his beard,
And trickled to the floor.   At each fresh draught

New vigor seemed to nerve his agèd limbs,
And he sat more erect, and lifted up
His trembling voice and sang an ancient song.
The vaulted roof re-echoed with the shouts
Of the mad revellers when the song was o'er,
And eagerly they called out, " Sing again ! "
The old man took another draught of wine,
And, smiling, once again essayed to sing.
It was a love-song,—a sweet, simple thing,—
A song he oft had sung in his fresh youth,
When his young heart was gay as any bird's,
And life was like a glorious dream of flowers.
His trembling voice grew stronger as he sang,
And his hard features softened, and a smile
Played o'er his face, and in his glistening eye
A tear-drop stood.   His inmost soul was stirred
With thoughts of other days, and his harsh voice
Grew soft as woman's, and his radiant face
Beamed with the light of tender memories.
But suddenly his cheek turned deadly pale,
And he fell backward, with his long lean hand
Pressed to his side, as if in sudden pain.
The guests, alarmed, ran quickly to his aid,
And raised him up, and pressed a brimming cup
Against his lips.   But with a gesture he
Put it away, and lifting up his head,
Spake in a solemn voice, unlike his own,
While the dazed revellers stood silent by :

      " Nay, tempt me not again!
I will not touch the wine-cup in this hour—

Too often have I felt its deadly power;
    And I would clear my brain
In these last trembling moments, for I feel
Death's icy hand across my temples steal.

    " Nay, do not smile at me,
And mock me with false hope of many days ;
My time has come : this is death's filmy haze
    That will not let me see
Your faces round me, though the lamps are bright
And the wine glitters in the sparkling light.

    " To die in such a place!
I who once knelt beside my mother's knee
To say my evening prayer. And must it be
    That I may ne'er retrace
The pathway of my life, lest haply I
Might do one deed of good before I die?

    " And must I die to-night,
With the still echoing songs to mar my peace;
To bid all thoughts of heavenly subjects cease?
    Ere the sun's golden light
Streams through the windows of this awful place,
Death will have stamped his impress on my face.

    " Oh, listen to my voice,
Ye, who have often shouted with delight
At my rude jesting, listen now to-night.
    Ye, who in youth rejoice,
Be warned by me, and stay while yet 'tis time,
Ere your young souls get hardened unto crime.

"Oh, shun the wine-cup now!—
Now, while the light of youth is in your eye;
While hope weaves golden colors in your sky;
 Ere yet upon your brow
The frosts of winter fall, and Time's rough share
Plow, deep and lasting, bitter furrows there.

"I have been wont to sneer
At holy themes, and laugh at those who trod
The path of virtue and looked up to God
 With holy, reverent fear.
But now I would give worlds if I could pray
The prayer I would repeat at close of day.

"Raise my head higher now—
Open the windows, let me have more air,
I cannot breathe!—why do you wildly stare?
 This cold sweat on my brow
Is death, I know. I faint—I reel—I fall!
Mind my last words. Ha! may God save you all!"

His head fell back; and they who watched him die
Stood gazing at each other for awhile,
And then with soft, slow steps they one by one
Crept silently away. The banquet-hall
Is silent and deserted, and the walls
No longer echo to the revellers' mirth.
There is a solemn stillness in the place
As if the ghosts of the departed hours
Had found a refuge there. The owlet screams
About the windows; and the moonlight falls
Upon the empty board; and all is still.
       W. A. EATON.

WOMEN AND TEMPERANCE WORK.

AN old Quaker lady, in the time of the crusade,
went with a young woman into a rum-shop.
The saloon-keeper looked at them and said: "What
have you women come up here for?" and an old
lady of fourscore years looked up and said gently:
"I will tell thee what I came here for. Thee knows
I had five sons and many grandsons; thee knows
here at thy counter more than one of my boys tasted
his first glass; thee knows that more than one of
them has gone to the drunkard's grave, and one by
the suicide's knife; and can't thee let his mother
lay her Bible down on thy counter, where her boy
took that glass, and read to thee these words of
God: 'Woe unto him who putteth the bottle to his
neighbor's lips'?" That is what we have here in
America in the rum-shops, something that devas-
tates the places we care most for, ruins the destinies
of those we love best, have borne most for, and would
shield with most of tenderness. And we want to say
just this: We believe that we can do something about
it. I believe that you and I—you, young lady, you,
young man, you, young child, you, man and woman
of middle life, in the strength of your years—have
something to do about it. This is one thing we are
going to do: we are going to carry the Gospel to the
drinking class, the class that is most beyond the
pulpit's influence of any class. If we make an
advance all along the line, upon a body so numerous

we must call out the reserve force of the Church; and you know two-thirds of the church members are women, and we must call them out; they have had the most in jeopardy; they have suffered the most, and will put forth the most earnest efforts in this work. Then another thing: women as a class, and the women of the wealthier class, and those of the middle class, are not so worn out and tugged out all their lives with care and anxiety as men; they have more leisure. That is something that will bear demonstration.

You and I are learning that not in the acquisition of a language, not in the mastery of a piano keyboard, lies the supreme good; but in teaching the tender feet never to stray from the sure path, and in going out to seek him who is "away in the mountains bleak and bare, away from the tender Shepherd's care." There it lies more than anywhere else on earth, and we are getting to believe it. Those who have been on tours of philanthropy, these Christian women, are getting more of an idea of making it a business. We have tasted the sweetness of benignant life. The truest, most nutritious food God has given us we find in well-doing. I think about it what a fine thing it is to know a language, and many of us will never know any but our mother tongue, but yet there are none here but can learn and teach the words of life, the language of Canaan. We may not be able to obtain the highest proficiency in mathematics; but you and I can help many a tangled, wicked life into a plain solution. It is a tender thing to be a sculptor and to chisel marble into beautiful shapes and forms, but it is sweeter to mold the clay of a child's character. It is a noble thing to be an architect and build grand cathedrals; but grander far to teach somebody who had not found it out, that the body and the soul were made on purpose to be the temple of the Holy Ghost, in which shall dwell nothing that is not pure and white and clean. It is a grand thing, surely, to be able to trace upon the canvas features of beauty, but ah! to restore the image of God to the face that is really the face that smiles back into your own, to restore there the image of God, which was lost, that is a better office; and to sweep the harps Æolian, to strike the keys that tune with God's purpose in creation, that is a nobler kind of music than any ever learned from Beethoven or Mozart. That is for you, for me, and for every one of us, blessed be God's name.

FRANCES E. WILLARD.

DARE TO STAND ALONE.

BE firm, be bold, be strong, be true,
    And dare to stand alone;
Stand for the right whate'er ye do,
    Though helpers there be none.

Nay, bend not to the swelling surge
    Of popular sneer and wrong;

'Twill bear thee on to ruin's verge
  With current wild and strong.

Stand for the right!   Humanity
  Implores, with groans and tears,
Thine aid to break the festering links
  That bind her toiling years.

Stand for the right!   Though falsehood reign,
  And proud lips coldly sneer,
A poisoned arrow cannot wound
  A conscience pure and clear.

Stand for the right, and with clean hands
  Exalt the truth on high!
Thou'lt find warm, sympathizing hearts
  Among the passers-by—

Men who have seen, and thought, and felt,
  And yet could hardly dare
The battle's brunt, but by thy side
  Will every danger share.

Stand for the right! proclaim it loud!
  Thou'lt find an answering tone
In honest hearts, and thou no more
  Be doomed to stand alone.

"NO SALOONS UP THERE."

DEAD!
  Dead in the fullness of his manly strength, the
ripeness of his manly beauty, and we who loved him
were glad.

His coffin rested on his draped piano, his banjo and his flute beside it. And as we looked on his brown curls thrown up from the cold white brow, on his skilled hands folded on his breast, on his sealed lips, of which wit and melody had been the very breathings, the silence was an awe, a weight upon us, yet our voiceless thanks rose up to God that he was dead.

Always courteous in manner, kind in word, obliging in act; everybody liked Ned, the handsome, brilliant Ned.

Three generations of ancestors, honorable gentlemen all, had taken the social glass as gentlemen, but never lowered themselves to drunkenness; but their combined appetite they had given as an heirloom to Ned, and from his infancy he saw wine offered to guests at the dinner parties, and, when he had been "a perfect little gentleman," was given by his father one little sip.

He grew and the taste grew, and when his father was taken, all restraint but a mother's love was taken.

As the only son of a praying mother, now the church would hold him up, now the saloon would draw him down; now his rich voice would join his mother's to swell the anthems of the church, now make the night hideous with his ribald songs. So all along the years he was her idol and her woe.

When her last sickness was upon her, the mother said to a friend:

"They tell me when I am gone Eddie will go

down unchecked, that in some wild spree or mad delirium he will die. But he will not. His fathers created the appetite they gave my poor boy. His disgrace is their sin, and my sin, too. He saw it on our table, tasted it in our ice-creams, jellies and sauces. For this my punishment is greater than I could bear but for the sure faith that God has forgiven me and will answer my daily, nightly prayers, and Eddie will die an humble penitent. It is just that I be forbidden to enjoy here the promised land, but I know whom I believe, and my boy will be carried safely over."

As death drew nigh every breath was a prayer for "Eddie," and as he chafed her death-cold hands the pallid lips formed the words no ear could catch, "Meet—me—in—heaven." And his voice, rich and full, responded, "I will, mother—I will."

And as from her mountain height of faith and love she caught a sight of that "promised land," with a seraph's smile she whispered, "I—thank Thee—O Father," and was gone.

And his uncontrollable grief made one say to another, "His mother's death will be his salvation."

He covered the new-made grave with flowers, and when others had left the cemetery he went back and sat beside it until nightfall, and then went to his lone home, and the oppressive silence drove him out to walk. He passed a saloon; some of his old associates came out and said kind words of sympathy. His soul was dark and sad, and from the open door came light and cheerful voices, and he went in.

Before the long spree was over he bade a crony "Take that old book out of my sight."

That old book ! the Bible he had seen his sainted mother reading morning, night, and often mid-day, and from which he had read to her those suffering, dying days.

Then a friend of his mother took him to her home and brought him back to soberness, remorse and a horror of himself. For months he did nobly and became active in Christian work, and refused all the urging to "just step in and see your old friends," and we felt there was joy in heaven.

Then he was asked to bring his banjo and sing at an oyster supper at the most respectable saloon in town, where "no one is ever asked to drink."

A wild spree was the result, and his robe was so mired he doubted if it had been white. And he lost hope, lost faith in himself, and worse, lost faith in God.

Kind arms were thrown about him, and again he was placed upon his feet. Very humble, very weak, he tried once more to walk the heavenward path.

"I am very glad to see you so well," I said one day when I met him.

"I don't know how long it will last," he said, sadly.

"Forever, I hope," I said, cheerily.

"I shall try hard to have it, but there will come an unguarded moment—but you know nothing about it."

Some two weeks after I met a physician.

"I have a case for you ladies. Ned is very sick."

" Has liquor anything to do with it?"

"No, not all. He has pneumonia, but his old drinking has so ruined his stomach it will go hard with him."

His nurse told us he thought he would die, and constantly exclaimed: " My wasted life! my wasted life! God cannot forgive it." He would fear to die, and pray to live to redeem his past; then he would fear to live, and pray to be taken away from temptation. So wore on a week, and then he gave up self and grew calm in Christ.

One Sunday he said his mother was in the room and wondered we could not see her, and with a smile on his face, and "mother" on his lips he passed beyond.

As I came out of the house one of his whilom associates, sober and sad, took off his hat and asked, " Is it all over?"

Impressed with the vast meaning of these two little words, I bowed and answered back:

" All over!"

With a voice full of pathos he said:

" The dear fellow is all right now. There are no saloons up there."

I walked on, repeating to myself: " No saloons up there! Thy will be done on earth as it is in heaven."

BALTIMORE METHODIST.

THE TESTIMONY OF EXPERIENCE.

FOR nearly two hundred years license has had possession of the entire field. But no one can affirm it has repressed intemperance. This is the point—the very pivot—of the question between license and Prohibition. License means liquor, and liquor means drunkenness. Drunkenness is seen everywhere. It meets you in the streets and on the highways, in railroad trains, and, sad but true, too often under their wheels. You see it at clubs and dinners, at celebrations and public meetings. It is found in lockups, mayor's offices, and court-rooms. No place is exempt from its curse. Who does not know that license, high or low, means to sell, and sales mean intoxication? Look at your morning papers—they are the diurnal records of vice, folly, crime, infamy, and injury resulting from the sales of liquor. Their location is the bar-room and the saloon, where nightly orgies outrage all decency, and deadly brawls end in bloodshed and murder.

The act of 1887 (the so-called Brooks High License Law,) is a license law, and can never rise above its own purpose and nature, viz., the sale of liquors; and sales mean drinking, drinking means intoxication, and intoxication runs into fighting, brawls, lewdness and bloodshed; and these mean lockups, the work-house, jail, penitentiary, poor-houses, and insane asylums. All these mean private woe and ruin, and public wrongs, expense, burdens, and taxation, running far above all that the highest-price license can repay.

Surely the instruction of experience magnifies the wisdom of this declaration of the board of bishops of the M. E. Church, that "the liquor traffic is so pernicious in all its bearings, so inimical to the interests of honest trade, so repugnant to the moral sense, so injurious to the peace and order of society, so hurtful to the homes, to the church and to the body politic, and so utterly antagonistic to all that is precious in life, that the only proper attitude toward it for Christians is that of relentless hostility. It can never be legalized without sin. No temporary device for regulating it can become a substitute for Prohibition. License, high or low, is vicious in principle, and powerless as a remedy."

Consider now the testimony of experience to the success of Prohibition, and choose this day which gives the surest promise of quick and permanent relief from the liquor curse.

In his message to the Legislature of Kansas on January 8, 1889, Governor John A. Martin makes the following plain and unequivocal statements in regard to the practical results of the Prohibitory Laws of that State:

"There is no longer any issue or controversy in Kansas concerning the results or beneficence of our temperance laws. Except in a few of the larger cities, all hostility to them has disappeared. For six years, at four exciting general elections, the questions involved in the abolition of the saloon were disturbing and prominent issues, but at the election held in November last, this subject was rarely mentioned by partisan speakers or newspapers. Public opinion, it is plainly apparent, has undergone a marked change, and there are now very few citizens in Kansas who would be willing to return to the old order of things.

"The change of sentiment on this question is well grounded and natural. No observing and intelligent citizen has failed to note the beneficent results already attained. Fully nine-tenths of the drinking and drunkenness prevalent in Kansas eight years ago have been abolished; I affirm, with earnestness and emphasis, that this State is to-day the most temperate, orderly, sober community of people in the civilized world. The abolition of the saloon has not only promoted the personal happiness and general prosperity of our citizens, but it has enormously diminished crime; has filled thousands of homes, where vice and want and wretchedness once prevailed, with peace, plenty and contentment; and has materially increased the trade and business of those engaged in the sale of useful and wholesome articles of merchandise. Notwithstanding the fact that the population of the State is steadily increasing, the number of criminals confined in our penitentiary is steadily decreasing. Many of our jails are empty, and all show a marked falling-off in the number of prisoners confined. The dockets of our courts are no longer burdened with long lists of criminal cases. In the Capital District, containing a population of nearly sixty thousand, not a single criminal case was on the docket when the present term began. The business of the police courts of our larger cities has dwindled to one-fourth of its former proportions, while in the cities of the second and third class the occupation of police authorities is practically gone. These suggestive and convincing facts appeal alike to the reason and the conscience of the people. They have reconciled those who doubted the success, and silenced those who opposed the policy of prohibiting the liquor traffic."

THE PRESENT CRISIS.

Permission of Houghton, Mifflin & Co.

WHEN a deed is done for freedom, through the
    broad earth's aching breast
Runs a thrill of joy prophetic, trembling on from
    East to West;
And the slave where'er he cowers, feels the soul
    within him climb
To the awful verge of manhood, as the energy sublime
    lime
Of a century bursts full-blossomed on the thorny
    stem of Time.

Through the walls of hut and palace shoots the instantaneous throe,
    stantaneous throe,

When the travail of the ages wrings earth's systems
    to and fro;
At the birth of each new era, with a recognizing
    start,
Nation wildly looks on nation, standing with mute
    lips apart,
And glad Truth's yet mightier man-child leaps be-
    neath the future's heart.

For mankind are one in spirit, and an instinct bears
    along,
Round the earth's electric circle, the swift flash of
    right or wrong;
Whether conscious or unconscious, yet humanity's
    vast frame
Through its ocean-sundered fibres, feels the gush of
    joy or shame;
In the gain or loss of our race, all the rest have
    equal claim.

Once to every man and nation, comes the moment
    to decide
In the strife of truth with falsehood, for the good or
    evil side
Some great cause, God's new Messiah, offering each
    the bloom or blight,
Parts the goats upon the left hand, and the sheep
    upon the right,
And the choice goes by forever 'twixt that darkness
    and that light.

Hast thou chosen, O my people, in whose party thou
    shalt stand,
Ere the doom from its worn sandals shakes the dust
    against our land?
Though the cause of evil prosper, yet 'tis truth
    alone is strong;
And albeit she wander outcast now, I see around her
    throng
Troops of beautiful tall angels, to enshield her from
    all wrong.

We see dimly in the present, what is small and what
    is great;
Slow of faith, how weak an arm may turn the iron
    helm of fate!
But the soul is still oracular—amid the market's din,
List the ominous stern whisper from the delphic
    cave within:
" They enslave their children's children, who make
    compromise with sin."

'Tis as easy to be heroes, as to sit the idle slaves
Of a legendary virtue carved upon our fathers'
    graves;
Worshipers of light ancestral make the present light
    a crime.
Was the *Mayflower* launched by cowards? steered
    by men behind their time?
Turn those tracks toward past or future that make
    Plymouth Rock sublime?

They were men of present valor—stalwart old icono-
    clasts—
Unconvinced by axe or gibbet that all virtue was the
    past's;
But we make their truth our falsehood, thinking
    that has made us free;
Hoarding it in mouldy parchments, while our tender
    spirits flee
The rude grasp of that great impulse which drove
    them across the sea.

New occasions teach new duties.   Time makes
    ancient good uncouth;
They must upward still and onward, who would
    keep abreast of truth;
Lo, before us gleam her camp-fires!   We ourselves
    must pilgrims be,
Launch our *Mayflower*, and steer boldly through the
    desperate winter sea,
Nor attempt the future's portal with the past's
    blood-rusted key.

JAMES RUSSELL LOWELL.

UNDRESSING LITTLE NED.

"WHERE is 'Whisky Bill," who used to drive
that old white horse in front of a twenty-
five-cent express wagon?" repeated the man in tones
of surprise.

" Yes, I want to know."

" Well, now, it is a curious case," he slowly continued ; " we all thought he had gone to the dogs,
for sure he was drinking a pint of whisky a day ; but
a few months ago he braced right up, stopped drinking, and now I hear he's in good business and saving
money. It beats all, for the last time I saw him he
seemed half under ground."

When you go home at night and find that all's
well with your flesh and blood, do you go to bed
reasoning that the rest of the world must take care
of·itself? Do you ever shut your eyes and call up
the hundreds of faces you have met during the day,
and wonder if the paleness of death will cover any
of them before the morrow? When you have once
been attracted to a face, even if it be a stranger's,
do you let it drop from memory with your dreams,
or do you call it up again and again, as night
comes down, and hope it may not lose any of its
brightness in the whirling mists of Time?

So " Whisky Bill" was hunted up. An inquiry
here and there finally traced him to a little brown
cottage on a by-street. He sat on the step in
the twilight, a burly, broad-shouldered man of
fifty, and in the house three or four children
gathered around the lamp to look over a picture-
book.

" Yes, they used to call me 'Whisky Bill' down
town," he replied, as he moved along and made
room, " but it is weeks since I heard the name. No
wonder they think me dead, for I've not set my

eyes on the old crowd for months, and don't want to for months to come."

"They tell me you have quit drinking. But one could see that by your face."

"I hope so. I haven't touched a drop since February. Before that I was half drunk day in and day out, and more of a brute than a man. I don't mind saying that my wife's death set me to thinking, but it didn't stop my liquor. God forgive me ! but I was drunk when she died, half drunk at the grave, and I meant to go on a regular spree that night. It was low down, sir, but I was no better than a brute those days."

"And so you left your motherless children at home, went out, and got drunk?"

"No, I said I meant to, but I didn't. The poor things were crying all day, and after coming home from the burial I thought to get 'em tucked away in bed before I went out. Drunk or sober, I never struck one of my children, and they never ran from me when I staggered home. There's four of 'em in there, and the youngest is not quite four years yet. I got the oldest ones to bed all right, and then came little Ned. He had cried himself to sleep, and he called for mother as soon as I woke him. Until that night I never had that boy on my knee, to say nothing of putting him to bed, and you can guess these big fingers made slow work with the hooks and buttons. Every minute he kept saying mother didn't do this ; and the big children were hiding their heads under the quilts to drown their sobs. When I had the clothes off and his night-gown on, I was ashamed—broke down; and when the oldest saw the tears in my eyes, and jumped out of bed to put her arms around my neck, I dropped the name of 'Whisky Bill' right then and there forever."

"And little Ned?"

"May be I'd have weakened but for him," replied the man, wiping his eyes.

"After I got the child's night-gown on, what did he do but kneel right down beside me and wait for me to say the Lord's Prayer to him! Why, sir, you might have knocked me down with a feather! There I was, mother and father to him, and I couldn't say four words of that prayer to save my life! He waited and waited for me to begin, as his mother always had; and the big children were waiting; and when I took him in my lap and kissed him, I called Heaven to witness that my life should change from that hour. And so it did, sir, and I have been trying hard to lead a sober, honest life. God helping me, no one shall call me 'Whisky Bill' again."

The four children, little Ned in his night-gown, came out for a good-night kiss, and the boy cuddled in his father's arms for a moment, and said:

"Good-night, pa—good-night everybody in the world—good-night ma up in heaven—and don't put out the light till we get to sleep."

STEPPING IN FATHER'S TRACKS.

ALL through night's wearying darkness snowy
  flakes
In eddying whirls had filled the wintry air;
As noiselessly as Time our blossoms takes
  They drifted here and there.
And when the glowing, rosy-hearted morn
  Awoke earth's sleeping denizens anew,
Behold! the snow upon the night-winds borne
  Had buried streets and lanes from view.
The city hosts assailed the crested snow,
  And, as the Red Sea waves of old rolled back,
Foam-banks on every side loomed up, and lo!
  All walked a solid track.
But yonder farm-house, like a ship at sea
  Becalmed with all sails set, awoke to hear
The low of kine, flocks bleating to be free,
  The while the day drew near.

The farmer, anxious for his troubled herd,
  With sturdy stride the trackless snow-drifts passed;
By their great need to strong exertion spurred,
  He reached the fold at last.
His gladsome son, exulting, darted on,
  Swift as an arrow from an archer's bow;
" I'll go," he shouted, " where my father's gone;
  I care not for the snow!"
He stumbled, struggled, fell; yet still he tried,
  For pride or courage stayed his turning back,
Until a new thought dawned. " I'll go!" he cried;
  " I'll step in father's track."

How many glorious victories have been won,
  How many from temptation have turned back,
Defying evil, just because a son
  Would step in father's track!
How should you walk, O father! lest too late
  You strive to call some erring wanderer back?
For precepts best on these examples wait
  That leave the brightest track.
So live that when the deepening snows of age
  Shall hold your failing strength in bondage back,
Your childrens' best and noblest heritage
  Shall be your shining track.
And when the household and the hearth are gone,
  And tender looks and tones may not come back,
Your mantle long may rest upon the son
  Who steps in " father's track."

LOUISE S. UPHAM.

EXTRACT FROM A SPEECH ON TEMPER-ANCE.

I HAVE come before you this beautiful Sabbath afternoon not to speak to you about political parties nor about the details of legislation. I come to speak to you, if possible, heart to heart, soul to soul, not to denounce, but if possible, to persuade. I come not to demand, but to plead with every one of you. I come to speak for that liberty which makes us free; that liberty which elevates body and soul above the thraldom of the intoxicating cup.

We have passed through scenes that have rocked this land to its centre, on the question whether human slavery should continue on our soil. It was but the slavery of the body. It was but for this life. But the slavery against which I speak to-day is the slavery of not only soul and body and talent and heart for this life, but is a slavery which goes beyond the gates of the tomb to an unending eternity.

We speak of the horrors of war, and there are horrors in war. Carnage, and bloodshed, and mutilation, and broken frames, and empty sleeves, and widows' weeds, and children's woes, and enormous debts and grinding taxation, all come from war, though war may be a necessity for saving a nation's life. But it fails in all its horrors, compared with those that flow from intoxication. We shudder at the ravages of pestilence, and famine, but they sink into insignificance when compared with the sorrow and anguish that follow in the train of this conquerer of fallen humanity.

I see before me many distinguished in political, social and business life; and some of them I fear are to-day voluntarily enrolled in the great army of moderate drinkers. When you appeal to them to give the force of their influence and example to the prevention of the evil, their answer is, that they have strength to resist, they can quit when they please. Possibly they can; but before you all I can frankly acknowledge, from what I have seen in public and private life, that I dare not touch or taste or handle the wine bowl. You say you are strong. I can point you to those stronger tenfold over than you, who began as you have, and who lost the power of resistance before they knew they were in the power of the tempter. This demon, like death, seems to love a shining mark. He only is fortified who has determined not to yield to the first temptation.

There is but one class whence he has never drawn a victim. That class has defied him, and will to the end. It is we who stand, God helping us, with our feet on this rock of safety, against which the waves may dash, but they shall dash in vain. I implore you to come and stand with us. I plead with you to come, for I believe that all mankind are my brethren. I believe in the fatherhood of God and in the brotherhood of man. And when I see an inebriate reeling along the streets I feel that, though debased and fallen, he is my brother still, created in the image of God, destined to an eternal hereafter; and it should be your duty and mine to take him by the hand and seek to place his feet on the same rock on which we stand.

That is what gave such a wonderful triumph to the Washingtonians, this recognizing the duty of individual responsibility. How many of you have gone to your fellow-man when you have seen him on the shore of destruction and tried to save him? Not one! Not one! How dare you on your knees ask God to bless you and yours, when you have not thus proved that you love your neighbor as yourself! This duty should be impressed on your souls by your ministers in the pulpit, by your writers in the public press. More than all things else in the land we need a temperance revival. Whom would it harm? No one.

But come down to the individual home of the man who has become a slave to this demon. Do you find happiness there? Do you find contentment, prosperity? Ah, no. Do you find the wife's cheek lighting up with joy as her husband comes home when the shadows lengthen? Ah, no: her cheek pales at the step of him who pledged her a life of devotion for the love she gave to him. All things are warning you to beware of yielding to this evil. The scriptures; the men reeling in their cups; your poor-houses; your prisons; the forsaken wives; all cry "beware." In the language of an eminent champion of temperance, "When drink can easily be given up by you, give it up for the sake of your example on others; if it be difficult to give it up, give it up for your own sake."

Choose you this day whether you will stand with us on this rock, defying the snares, and evil, and misery, and woe, and desolation of the tempter, or whether, pursuing your present habit, you will go down the easy descent, till at last, dishonored and disgraced, having lost the respect of others and your own self-respect, you end a miserable and gloomy life by a home in the tomb, from which there is, if inspiration be true, no resurrection that shall take you to a better land.

SCHUYLER COLFAX.

THE MULTITUDE OF LITTLES.

THERE is no pleasure like the pleasure of doing good. Oh, the joy of being instrumental in leading some poor sinner from the error of his ways! How much of our work perishes! How much there will be in a year's time, when we think of it, that we will wish we had not spent any money or time or labor upon it! But nobody will regret the work he has done for God and for his fellow-creatures. No one will ever regret any sacrifice of money or of time expended in restoring the poor prodigal, and leading into the way of righteousness those who have erred and strayed from it. Let us all try and do something, and do not let us be deterred from doing anything because we can only do a little. The great ocean is made up of little drops. Your great army was made up of single men, and if one man had said, "I won't enlist, because I am only one," where would have been your army, your Union, and your universal liberty? The most beneficent agencies that visit our physical world come in little things. The rain that fertilizes the earth, in what little drops it comes! And so God compares with these the inestimable blessings of His grace. "My doctrine shall distil as the dew. My speech shall come down as the rain, as the small rain upon the tender herb, as the showers upon the grass." Do not despise the day of small things. Our influence, if not exerted for what is good, may be exerted for what is bad; and our little influence may go to augment the greatness of something that is bad, as well as of that which is good. We may not be able ourselves to do some great thing, but we may put forth a little effort toward accomplishing a great result, which is achieved only by the multiplication of littles; and so, by our neglect, we may do a little toward the propagation of enormous evil. What a little thing is a flake of snow! Watch it, flying backward and forward, long before it can settle. Look up yonder on those mountain slopes, where some of you love to wander. The snow falls there during the months of winter, flake by flake, each so small and gentle; but the avalanche is gathering, and that vast snow-field is falling. Now as the spring advances, the sun gets a little hotter, and the snow gets a little looser; at the bottom there is some .little influence added to preceding influences. Now the avalanche is in motion, slowly at first, and now, with rapidly accelerated speed, it descends—it over-leaps the chasm, sweeps away the pine forest, thunders down the glen, and overwhelms the village. That avalanche was made up of single flakes of snow. So is it with the avalanche of drunken-ness and irreligion which is sweeping through the world, and destroying tens of thousands of precious lives, and the souls of immortal beings—the eloquent man, the cunning artificer, the prattling child, the daring youth, the delicate maiden, and the tender woman! Oh, what multitudes are being hurried down to destruction by this terrible avalanche of

drunkenness that is made up of little things!—the
single glass of the moderationist, as well as the
twenty glasses of the drunkard; champagne as well
as gin; the polite banquet, as well as the rude revel;
the approving smile of the virtuous lady, as well as
the drunken shriek of the abandoned outcast! I
call upon you, my friends, to unite your energies,
however feeble they may be, not to augment the
murderous avalanche of intemperance, ignorance,
and wickedness, but to come down as the small rain
and tender dew of temperance and godliness.

REV. NEWMAN HALL.

THE NEW EMANCIPATION.

O GREAT Republic, rise and shake
  Thyself! thine iron fetters break,
For thou art bound; thy statesmen fail,
With brain and heart too weak! they quail
Before the oligarchic throng
That build their bulwarks strong.
    Arise, O Nation!
Declare a new emancipation.

The drink-lords, scarlet-vested, hold
Their titles bought with yellow gold,
And laugh to see the nation reel
With burdens which they scorn to feel;
They hold the keys of power, and faint
The nation grows without complaint;

An outlaw rises
And smites the land which he despises.

Have we a heart American,
O citizens! the rights of man
We boast as our inheritance,
From shore to shore a wide expanse,
And point to our exultant stars
O'er mountain crags and harbor bars,
        And here a giant
Holds sway against all laws defiant.

The great Rotunda's shadow falls
Ashamed upon his carnivals!
Hark! down the Treasury vaults it rolls
The " fifty millions " which controls;
Ah, yes, ye statesmen! this is why
The outlaw ye will not deny;
        He pays in millions
And revels in you broad pavilions.

Think ye the great Republic still
Will grow beneath this load of ill?
The earthquake underneath us lies;
The thunderbolt is in the skies;
Columbia, grapple with thy curse,
Or see thy chariot wheels reverse,
        Thy glory fading,
And for thy sin thyself upbraiding!

Where is the coming citizen,
Whose hand shall grasp the patriot pen,

And write the edict strong and grand
Which shall emancipate the land,
And crush the oligarch of drink?
When men shall act as now they think,
    And all united
Shall chase away the curse affrighted.
       REV. DWIGHT WILLIAMS.

A WISE RESOLUTION.

SHALL I ever be a drunkard
  Like the poor men that we meet
Reeling, staggering, tottering, mumbling,
  Falling helpless in the street?
Will the boys leave off their playing,
  Run in fright when I come near?
No! I'll never drink the poison,
  Then I never need to fear.

Shall I ever be a drunkard,
  With a base, dishonored name,
Shrinking from the good and virtuous
  In defiance or in shame?
Face all bloated, clothes all ragged,
  Out at elbows, out at toes?
No! I'll never drink the poison,
  Then I'll never know its woes.

Shall I ever be a drunkard—
  Can that—will that ever be?

For the very men I pity
  Once were little boys like me.
Some of them ne'er dreamed that ever
  They should bear the drunkard's name.
But I'll never taste the poison,
  Then I'll never feel the shame.

Shall I ever be a drunkard?
  Never! By God's helping grace,
In the noble ranks of Temperance
  I will keep a foremost place.
Others may sip drops of brandy,
  Porter, whiskey, gin, or beer,
But I'll never touch the poison,
  Then I'll never need to fear.

                              E. C. A. ALLEN.

SIGNALS OF DISTRESS!

'TIS very sad to see a tear bedim a loved one's eye,
    To see a cherished bosom heave an anguish-
      laden sigh:
'Tis sad to see the cheeks grow pale where once was
      health's rich bloom,
To see the brightness fade from eyes, 'neath sorrow's
      heavy gloom;
'Tis sad to see a youthful face wearing a transient
      smile,
And know the throbbing heart with pain is sorely
      charged the while.

Yes, it is sad to know of hearts oppressed with heavy
woes,
But sadder still to see the bloom upon a drunkard's
nose.

It tells of good name, credit gone; of time and
talents wasted;
Of joys, of friendship, love, and home, all thrust
aside untasted.
For glowing health and peaceful sleep, and waking
hours of gladness,
It says he has exchanged remorse, disease, unrest,
and sadness;
The drunken brawl, an aching head, and garments
soiled and rent,
For decent clothing, wholesome food, and unalloyed
content.
Exposed to insult, mockery, and scorn where'er he
goes,
There is no signal of distress worse than a drunkard's nose.

ROBERT CROMPTON.

CONSTITUTIONAL PROHIBITION THE GREAT REMEDY.

I STAND here to say the experience of all these
years proves that the legislature is no place to
deposit discretionary power in dealing with the alcoholic liquor traffic. The power exercised by the

legislature is the people's power delegated by the people to the legislature; and the people have the right to recover any right or power which they have delegated whenever they think they can better their condition by so doing. The change will be that the people will say what the public policy shall be, and direct the legislature to make the principle in the organic law operative by functional law. If the principle does not prove practical, the people can at any time change it, but it can never be changed until the people will it.

So long as discretionary power is vested in the legislature, the drunkard-makers will annually use thousands of dollars if necessary to prevent right action; and when discretionary power is taken from them, one of the worst sources of legislative corruption will be dried up, because the legislature can act in but one way, and it will be useless to try to bribe them. With prohibition a settled principle in the Constitution, every legislator who swears to support the Constitution must vote in favor of a prohibitory law, making the principle operative, or be a perjurer and rebel.

I am aware that some will object that the Constitution is no place to define what shall and what shall not be crimes. The Constitution lays down principles of government, and to attack or violate those principles is a crime against the Constitution and the government. The defining and adopting the principles makes its violation a crime against the government. To adopt a constitutional amendment prohibiting the liquor traffic, is to make the principle of prohibition fundamental, and to change the spheres of authority to conform to the newly adopted principle. This was done in regard to African slavery. The people adopted the principle that no slavery should exist in the States, and left to Congress and the legislatures of the States the power to enact functional laws to carry out the will of the people.

The people of Iowa, finding lotteries dangerous to their best interests, declared it a fundamental principle of their government that lotteries should not exist; and the State has not been cursed with them since the principle was adopted by the people. When the people become convinced that a principle is right, the place for it is in the Constitution. That there are objections to changes in constitutions I am aware; but they are not as strongly urged as were the objections to written constitutions supplanting the unwritten ones. The constitution that cannot develop is a fraud, and a good basis for a despotism. To the objection that the amendment specifies a single institution, the answer is, that this institution is a special evil which is threatening the life of the government by debauching and degrading the units of the government. The question of its overthrow is the question of the existence or non-existence of republican institutions; and that the prohibition of the existence of such an institution is fundamental to the existence of the government it jeopardizes, is self-evident.

You are the ones who are to say what you will do with the matter, and I can only urge upon you the necessity of doing something. The duty of the hour is action, and the leaders should be in the front of the fight. Inaction and idleness produce the same results as treason to the principle. The liquor interests are active and aggressive, and the defenders of the home should be equally so.

What we want is men and women who, for the love of home and country, will enter the struggle to win; and after carefully studying the plan of action, draw the sword and throw away the scabbard, determined to only cease the struggle when victory comes to bless our homes and country.

JOHN B. FINCH.

WHAT LICENSE LEGALIZES.

HAVING recently had my saloons closed up in Kansas and Iowa, and appreciating the advantages of High License, I have moved over here and leased commodious rooms in Mr. Lovemoney's block, corner of Ruin street and Perdition lane (next door to the undertaker's), where I shall continue my business of manufacturing drunkards, paupers, lunatics, beggars, criminals and "dead beats" for sober and industrious people to support. Backed up by the law I shall add to the number of fatal accidents, of painful diseases, of disgraceful quarrels, of riots and of murders. My liquors are warranted to rob some of life; many of reason; most of property, and all of true peace; to make fathers fiends; wives, widows; children, orphans. I shall cause mothers to forget their infants; children to grow up in ignorance; young women to lose their priceless purity; young men to become loafers, swearers, gamblers, skeptics and "lewd fellows of the baser sort."

Boys and girls are the raw materials out of which I make drunkards, etc.; parents may help in this good work by always sending their children to buy the beer.

On two hours' notice I agree to put husbands in condition to reel home, break the furniture, beat their wives and kick their children out of doors; I shall also fit mechanics to spoil their work, be discharged and become tramps. If one of the regular customers should be trying to reform, I will for a few pennies take pleasure in inducing him again to take just one glass and start again on the road to destruction. The money which he has been wasting in bread and books for his children will buy luxuries for me. And when his money is gone, I will persuade him to run in debt, and then collect the bill by attaching his wages.

Orders promptly filled for fevers, scrofula, consumption or delirium tremens. In short, I agree to help bring upon all my customers, in this world, debt, disgrace, disease, despair and death, and in the next world the death that never dies.

Having closed my ears to God's warning voice,

having made a league with hell and sold myself to the devil, and having paid for my license, I have a right to bring all of the above evils upon my friends for the sake of gain.

Some have suggested that I display outside the door assorted specimens of my art. But that would blockade the street. A fine assortment of my manufactured wrecks may be seen inside, or at the city station-houses every morning, also in the poorhouse, the asylums, the prisons and on the gallows.

LIFE'S PURPOSE.

LIFE is not ours to waste it as we will;
  For high and noble ends a while 'tis lent;
And if we fail its purpose to fulfil,
  Whate'er we gain or lose, the time's misspent.
The talents God hath given, and bids us use;
  The which we should improve with all our care
His precious loan, alas! we oft abuse,
  And change His blessings to a hurtful snare.
Allured, deceived by pleasure's vain display,
  Through drink what myriads make their life a
    blot;
And in their sinful folly throw away
  Their highest good for that which profits not.
Life's purpose miss; rob God of all they might
  Have been and done, and perish in the night.

DAVID LAWTON.

THE TEMPERANCE STAR.

THE streets were rife with joyous life,
　For the Christmas time was near;
But into our rum-ruined home
　There crept no sign of cheer.

As I sat alone in the darkness,
　And looked through the coming years,
My heart was full of sorrow,
　And my eyes were full of tears.

Then I thought of the shepherds that kept their
　　flocks
On the plains of Galilee,
How their hearts sent up that longing cry
　For the Christ that was to be.

And I thought how the glory of God came down,
　Till the night shone like the day;
Of the wise men's journey by night, and the star
　That guided them all the way.

And my heart sent up its longing cry
　To the God who answered them;
" Lord, into the dark night of my life
　Send a Star of Bethlehem! "

I heard a step far down the walk—
　A firm and ringing tread:
It reminded me of John's glad step,
　The day that we were wed.

The moon slipped in and spread her robe
  Upon the poor bare floor,
Till I thought of the streets in the City of Light,
  And—John stood at the door!

There was a new light in his eyes,
  So tender and so proud;
And a ribbon shone on his ragged coat,
  Like a star against a cloud!

A little, silken, crimson star,
  That lighted all the gloom,
And changed to a palace, grand and fair,
  The dingy little room.

We did not speak a single word,
  But we knelt by the children's bed;—
"God help me to keep it always bright!"
  Was all the prayer he said.

The moon crept through the narrow pane,
  And fell like a blessing down;
It touched wee Mary's flaxen hair,
  Till it shone like a silver crown.

It kissed the baby where he lay,
  In his lowly cradle bed;
"Thank God for the Star that rose to-night!"
  Was all that my full heart said!

A THRILLING APPEAL.

A T a certain town-meeting the question came up whether any person should be licensed to sell liquor. The clergyman, the deacon, the physician, strange as it may now appear, all favored it. One man only spoke against it because of the mischief it did. The question was about to be put, when there arose from one corner of the room a miserable woman. She was thinly clad, and her appearance indicated the utmost wretchedness, and that her mortal career was almost closed. After a moment's silence, and all eyes being fixed on her, she stretched her attenuated body to its utmost height, and her long arms to their greatest length, and then raising her voice to a shrill pitch, she called all to look upon her. "Yes," she said, "look upon me, and then, hear me. All that the last speaker has said relative to temperate drinking as being the father of drunkenness, is true. All practice, all experience declare its truth. All drinking of alcoholic poison as a beverage in health, is excess. Look upon me! You all know me, or once did. You all know I was once mistress of the best farm in town; you all know, too, I had one of the best, the most devoted of husbands. You all know that I had five noble-hearted, industrious boys. Where are they now? Doctor, where are they now? You all know. You all know they lie in a row, side by side, in yonder churchyard; all—every one of them, filling the

drunkard's grave! They were all taught to believe
that temperate drinking was safe—that excess alone
ought to be avoided; and they never acknowledged
excess. They quoted you, and you, and you," pointing with her shred of a finger to the minister, deacon
and doctor, "as authority. They thought themselves safe under such teachers. But I saw the
gradual change coming over my family and its pros-
pects, with dismay and horror. I felt we were all
to be overwhelmed in one common ruin. I tried to
ward off the blow; I tried to break the spell, the
delusive spell, in which the idea of the benefits of
temperate drinking had involved my husband and
sons. I begged, I prayed; but the odds were against
me. The minister said the poison that was destroying my husband and boys was a good creature of
God; the deacon who sits under the pulpit there,
and took our farm to pay his rum bills, sold them
the poison; the doctor said a little was good, and the
excess only ought to be avoided. My poor husband
and my dear boys fell into the snare, and they could
not escape; and one after another were conveyed to
the sorrowful grave of the drunkard. Now look at
me again. You probably see me for the last time.
My sands have almost run. I have dragged my ex-
hausted frame from my present home—your poorhouse—to warn you all, to warn you, deacon, to warn
you, 'false teacher of God's word!'" and with her
arms flung high, and her tall form stretched to its
utmost, and her voice raised to an unearthly pitch,
she exclaimed: "I shall soon stand before the judg-

ment seat of God. I shall meet you there, you false guides, and be a witness against you all!"

The miserable woman vanished. A dead silence pervaded the assembly; the minister, the deacon, and physician hung their heads; and when the president of the meeting put the question, "Shall any licenses be granted for the sale of spirituous liquors?" the unanimous response was "NO!"

REINFORCEMENT.

WE are now in the gloaming, but the morning is
    breaking,
And upward the sun is intruding his ray.
The times point the hour to mankind for awakening
    And girding their loins for the work of the day.

We are not alone in our arduous labor,
    For thousands are watching the work that we do,
The service of God and the good of our neighbor
    Will draw to our ranks from the good and the
      true.

While we raise up our land to a better condition,
    And seek for the things which pertain to the
      right,
Let us work, in the hope of the blessed fruition
    When virtue and conscience shall reign in their
      might.

Prohibition must come, for the Lord has decreed it.
Nature and providence point to the day.
Jehovah has promised the gift when we need it,
And God and his providence never delay.

Prohibition is coming, for heroes of story
Look down from jasper and amethyst wall,
While martyrs and justified spirits in glory
Shout Glory to God, He shall reign over all.

Reinforcements are coming, from hill and from
mountain,
From down where the river flows into the sea,
And the valley is teeming, clear up to the fountain,
With the men who say that our land shall be free.

Reinforcements are coming where children are grow-
ing,
And temperance teaching is kept in the schools.
It surely can't be that the seed we are sowing
Will raise up a crop of political fools.

Reinforcements are coming. The women are banded,
The cohorts of home are combined for the fight.
'Tis a union of hearts, as their Lord has commanded,
To shut out the darkness and let in the light.

Reinforcements are coming; hark! hark! from the
mothers
Whose hearts have responded and come to the call.
The sisters arise to the help of their brothers
To free from their bondage and raise from their
fall.

The widows and orphans are viewing our labors,
  They smile when we triumph, and weep when we
    fail,
And victims of rum—our unfortunate neighbors—
  Are looking through bars from the prison and jail.

Inebriate souls who are slaves to their drinking,
  And hardly expect to obtain a release,
Are praying, when all that they dare is in thinking
  And longing for temperance, purity, peace.

The goddess of justice has banished her weapon,
  Her arm is now bare for the stroke of her brand.
Retribution is certain, whatever may happen,
  For justice shall rule in the laws of the land.

The spirit of evil come down from the ages,
  His dark, slimy track showing back all the way—
Approaches the doom which the prophets and sages
  Foretell should announce a prophetical day.

The mouths of the dragon are busy in sinning,
  His thoughts are alive with the satanic sport.
His power, though greater than at the beginning,
  Must cease; and he knows that his triumph is
    short.

The last reinforcement, a radiant angel,
  Descends with the chain of the law in his hand,
And temperance—part of the gospel evangel—
  Shall then be entrenched in the law of the land.

He will seize on the dragon, and banish his power,
   And with it our sorrow, and anguish, and tears.
We will shout hallelujah! to welcome the hour
   Which brings prohibition, a thousand bright years.

Then shout hallelujah! the Lord is descending,
   Millenial glories are coming to hand,
The reign of the dragon approaching its ending,
   For justice shall rule in the laws of the land.

LIBERTY.

LIBERTY is a dear word. And it is behind that good word, consecrated as it is by the memories of many a great struggle (for liberty is one of the things that men worthy of the name die for), it is behind that good word that our enemies, the saloon-keepers, have entrenched themselves. Liberty? Personal liberty? What liberty do they claim? Is it the liberty of the man in the midst of his family? A man will die for his wife, his little ones, for their custody, for the right to train them, to live with them, to educate them and be to them husband and father. Why, it is from the door of the saloon that the bloodstained footsteps are tracked that lead down to the destruction of the family. The idea of the men who keep saloons claiming liberty—liberty to poison the family; to breed in it dissensions, social warfare, the demon of the worst example!

They claim the liberty of the man—is that it? The liberty of that man is worse than that of one who would unlock the cage of wild beasts in the menagerie and turn them loose upon the little ones of your family and of every family in the land.

Then, there is another liberty that men claim—the liberty of the citizen. That is a great liberty, too. Now, is there anything like that sentiment of real civil liberty in that which inspires the saloonkeepers and their servants in the Legislature and the town council, that they should array themselves in Personal Liberty leagues, or that they should appeal to the general public, through the press and upon the platform, to the music of such a great word as that? They are the deadliest venom that poisons politics. It is from the doors of the saloon to the low caucus, and from the low caucus back to the saloon, that the footsteps are traced that mean the destruction of liberty; for they mean the destruction of all civil dignity and of all the honor of citizenship. We know that. Perhaps we know better than we can be told that, instead of their claiming any right of liberty because of citizenship, they are the ones who should be the most hated—if one could hate a person because of his vice—by those who love liberty and love citizenship.

There is just one other kind of liberty that men can claim—I believe it is the highest kind—and that is what is called "the liberty of religion." Of all truth that has rights and can claim liberty, religious truth stands first; for the more a man is filled with religion—that is to say, the more he is possessed of those truths which spur on, and those methods which actuate the noblest impulses of his being, in his dealings with all; and that is what religion is—the more fond he is of liberty in the state, the more capable he is of exercising safely and profitably the liberty of the man; for, after all, the end of religion is not simply restraint, the end of religion is not total abstinence, the end of temperance is not total abstinence; total abstinence, temperance, all restraint is a means to an end, and the end of all religion is animation, progress, a movement upward. It is a glimpse of the God-given power that is within us, of possessing the divine. It is the impulse that leads us forward and onward ever. It is religion, union with God, elevation. So that true religion, or even religion that may be mixed with error but which may have truth in it, in so far urges men on to liberty everywhere; and the liberty of the citizen follows the liberty of the Christian.

The man who has not his mind is as much worse than the slave as is the brute. It is the brutalizing of the man, and hence the imposing upon him of the brutish fetters of slavery, that makes the slavery of drink; and the slavery-making of the drunkard maker is the most detestable, hateful and deadly that is known. Liberty? Liberty forever—the liberty of the man; the liberty of the citizen; the liberty of conscience; the liberty of religion; always, forever;—more of it in greater and deeper draughts that liberty may enter into our very blood, that there may be less restraint upon the free limits of every man born in the image of God, but no liberty to do wrong, deadly wrong; no liberty to make slaves; no liberty to poison liberty; no liberty for the saloon-keeper.

REV. FATHER WALTER ELLIOTT.

OUR WARFARE AND OUR DUTY.

WE hold that all drinking of intoxicants is perilous and wrong, and that its influence upon others is very likely to be fatal to the drinker himself. Therefore, on principles of Scripture and common-sense, we war upon all use of intoxicating beverages, knowing that that deceitful thing or mocker makes a man believe he takes it moderately when he is on the high-road to ruin. We plant ourselves, therefore, on the immutable rock of total abstinence, and oppose the drinking of any intoxicants.

I would have the Church stand out as clear against the sin of the bottle and the curse of the dram-shop as it stands to-day against infidelity or superstition or crime of any kind. Why not? Is not drink the curse of curses? Why should the Church ignore it? Does it not lay its deadly hands on our boys and girls, husbands and wives, homes and hearts? How dare we, as Christians, turn a deaf ear to it, and wrap the mantle of our respectability about us, and pass on the other side while the victims of this curse lie bleeding on every side? God forbid! I would have every pulpit speak with no uncertain sound.

Moody never told a more timely truth than when in reply to a query sent up at a hall in Edinburgh, "How shall Scotland be delivered from intemperance?" he said: "Let every minister and church-member put the bottle off his own table." That single sentence set Scotland thinking. A while ago a Scotch minister was beguiled by his doctor (as I have known many a man in this community to be beguiled by his doctor) to take whiskey to break up some dyspeptic or other trouble. The minister said, "I can not do this." The doctor replied: "Yes, you can; you must take it hot; you may take it every morning in your room when the girl brings up the hot water to shave." He allowed his conscience to be salved and blistered; he tried whiskey, but he tried it rather too long. One of the elders called to know what had come over the minister. The man-servant, Jamie, replied: "I dinna ken what is the matter, but there is something wrong. Wad ye believe it, some days he is shaving himself all day, and all the while he is ringing and ringing for more hot water."

We want our ministers to give us a clear example wherever they go among the congregation, as well as to preach total abstinence from the pulpit. A minister cannot get a congregation higher commonly than his pulpit. If you smuggle a demijohn into a pulpit it will trickle out into every pew. Whenever the pulpit speaks distinctly for total abstinence, God honors such a ministry. He blessed them richly in the times gone by; He blesses them now and will evermore.

And these reformed men—my heart and my prayers are with them. I see them coming up out of the depth of misery, one after another, scarred and bruised and rough, many of them almost ruined. God's people are ready to put the arm of faith and prayer around them and welcome them, and these men feel, as long as the Divine Arm steadies their weak arms and the loving Jesus sustains their tempted hearts, they will stand. But, as Gough said: "I would give that right hand if I had never touched it." I do not want my boy to go through life with his arm in a sling, maimed and mangled; I want that boy's arm clear and sound. I want that boy saved, as your boy has got to be, by prevention. One ounce of prevention is worth a ton of cure. I honor the movement to save the drunkards. We have saved hundreds and thousands. The country is alive with great temperance meetings, and glorious results are accomplished by them. Let me say that, after all, it is not only the saving of drunkards we aim at, but it is the mighty work of prevention in keeping back thousands that would be tempted.

T. L. CUYLER, D. D.

SOMETHING TO HATE.

I LOVE the luscious grapes that cling,
  In clusters on the vine—
Bright groups of neckless bottles filled
  With nature's harmless wine.
But when, despoiled of all their charms,
  They fall to low estate,
Their sweetness into poison turned,
  I've something then to hate!

I love the apples, blushing 'neath
  The sun's too ardent rays;
They bring me pleasant memories of
  Dear childhood's happy days.
But when, by "Folly's" hand transformed,
  They lure and fascinate,
Their harmlessness and beauty gone,
  I've something then to hate!

I love the graceful barley, which,
  Disguised in beard of gold,
Goes flirting with the zephyrs like
  A cavalier of old;
But when the cruel hand of art
  Doth such a change create
That wholesome food's to poison turned,
  I've something then to hate.

PUT OUT THAT FIRE!

WHAT an enormous interest the drink-traffic has built up. They say in England, and with truth, that the drink-interest can turn an election over the country any day. I do not know but that it is true here, too. The power of it is tremendous. I am afraid to put an estimate upon how much money is sunk in it. And yet see how the law deals with it. You know that scene in "The Pilgrim's Progress;" it has a very beautiful spiritual meaning, and I am almost ashamed to take it out of its connection for the purpose for which I mean to employ it. You remember when Christian is in the house of Interpreter, and he sees a great blazing fire, and there are men trying all they can to put it out, but it blazes on in spite of all their efforts. He can not understand it; but Interpreter takes him round to the other side of the wall, where men are pouring in the oil, and then the whole thing is plain. That has a wonderful significance in the spiritual life; but do you not see the application of it here? Here are the licenses issued continually year by year for men to keep the fire up. Is it any wonder, therefore, that policemen, city missionaries, Bible-women, Scripture-readers, and temperance societies should all be frustrated in their attempts to put it out? Here we are all laboring to put out the fire, and the licensing principle is doing everything it can to pour in oil upon it and keep it up. And the worst of it is that the people love to have it so. The people think it is a grand thing to get that licensing money to support the public charities. How long is this anomaly and inconsistency. to continue in the midst of us? As long as the people permit it, and no longer. The responsibility is yours.

WILLIAM M. TAYLOR, D. D.

THE CUP-BEARER.

THE little cup-bearer entered the **room**,
  After the banquet was done;
His eyes were like the skies of May,
  All bright with a cloudless sun,
His hair a soft and wavy brown,
  His forehead white and high,
And his gentle voice and courteous mien
  Were a joy to every eye.

The little cup-bearer in his hand
  Carried a silver horn,
Wherein there flashed a rare old wine
  With a tint like the purple morn.
Kneeling beside his master's feet—
  The feet of the noble king—
He raised the goblet: " Drink, my liege,
  The offering that I bring!"

" Now, nay!" the good king, smiling, said.
  " But first—a faithful sign
That thou bringest me no poison draught,—
  Taste thou, my page, of the wine!"

Then sweet but gravely spoke the lad:
  "My dearest master, *no!*
Though at thy lightest wish my feet
  Shall gladly come and go."

"Rise up, my little cup-bearer!"
  The king astonished cried.
"Rise up and tell me straightway why
  Is my request denied?"
The young page rose up slowly,
  With sudden paling cheek,
While all the lords and ladies
  Waited to hear him speak.

"My father sat in princely halls,
  And tasted wine with you:
He died a wretched drunkard, sire!"
  (The brave voice tearful grew.)
"I vowed to my dear mother,
  Beside his dying bed,
That for her sake I would not taste
  The tempting poison red!"

"Away with this young upstart!"
  The lords impatient cry;
But, spilling slow the purple wine,
  The good king made reply:
"Thou shalt be my little cup-bearer,
  And honored well," he said;
"But see thou bring no wine to me,
  But water pure instead!"

A STORY OF SANTA CLAUS.

'TWAS Christmas Eve; the snow fell down
   In whirling eddies, borne around,
  Blown hither, thither, on the ground,
Above, all o'er the festive town.
With glee the rich man's children cried,
   "Oh, welcome snow! glad sport in store!"
  And watched the snow-storm from the door;
"Hard winter!" many a poor heart sighed.

The children's hearts beat gay and light;
   Gathered around the Christmas tree,
  Or on a parent's loving knee;
For Santa Claus would come to-night!
And dainty hands with loving care
   'Mid prattling of each childish tongue
  O'er downy pillows stockings hung,
That Santa Claus might find them there.

Oh, light and shade!   The artist hand
   Must mingle tints of every hue
  To paint a picture stern and true
The joys and miseries of a land.
Then turn to sorrow's haunt, thy gaze!
   A dim light o'er a garret thrown,
  A care-worn woman, who hath known
That saddening dream called "better days!"

Dragged down to drink-caused woes by him
   Whose vows of love her youth beguiled;
  A drunkard's wife, a drunkard's child
Are doomed to want and penury grim.

This night the mother's heart was wrung:
  She saw, by dim light, faintly shed,
  Oh, grief! beside her darling's bed
A little empty stocking hung!

And she had naught to fill it left!
  No little toy, for childish treat;
  No golden orange, juicy, sweet,
By him for drink, of all bereft!
She slept that night, 'twas misery's sleep,
  Till Christmas carols, sweet and clear,
  Broke in the morning on her ear;
Then she awoke to sigh and weep.

Her mother-heart gave one wild throb;
  She heard her darling's fingers grope
  Around the cot, in childish hope—
Then came a silence, and a sob!
It spoke of childish hopes all crushed,
  Of an awakening from a dream
  Bright with an almost fairy gleam,
It told of joy's song, rudely hushed!

Much grief the mother's heart had known,
  Hunger and cold and untold woe;
  But ne'er such anguish did she know
As wrung her heart that Christmas morn!
And this she felt grief's greatest sting
  Whate'er life's miseries or its woes
  None are so fierce, so dire as those,
Man on his fellow-man doth bring!

Oh, loving mother! tender wife,
　Whose hand upholds the wine-cup red,
　Yet seest no cause for future dread,
Know this—that wine with woe is rife!
He drank and fell, and thou dost blame;
　Hath not the cup the selfsame sting?
　When thou thy stone at him doth fling,
Remember! Thine may do the same!
　　　　　　　HARRIET A. GLAZEBROOK.

GAINING GROUND.

LET those laugh who will about it;
　　All their laughter is but sound.
Let who will pretend to doubt it;
　Still the cause is gaining ground.

Just so sure as yearly plowing
　Turns the furrow to the yield,
Just so sure as broadcast-sowing
　Brings a harvest to the field,

Just so sure all true endeavor,
　In despite of adverse fate,
Used in any line whatever,
　Brings an answer soon or late.

There is less of whisky-drinking,
　There's more deference to our cause;
There's more serious, quiet thinking
　On the subject than there was.

Do not think your star is waning,
Weary worker, never fear!
Yes, the cause is gaining, gaining,
Surely gaining year by year.

ELLA WHEELER WILCOX.

THE HOUSE FULL OF WINE.

A GAY little fly on a bright summer's morn
Went buzzing about 'mid the clover and corn,
Till, buzzed out of breath, he sat down on a flower,
And thought he would just take a nap for an hour.
A spider who built up a dwelling close by,
Just wanting a morsel to make up a pie,
Looking out of his window, delightedly sees
This fat little fly coolly taking his ease.
So he let himself down with his pulley and thread
Till he came to a leaf that was over his head,
And, speaking as kindly as ever he could,
Began to persuade him he'd come for his good.

"My dear little fly," said the spider above,
"I've a house full of wine and a heart full of love;
You're welcome to both, and I've just come to say
How glad I shall be of a visit to-day.
I fear you'll take cold from the damp of this flower;
There's room in my house, and I dine in an hour.
Take hold of my arm, you have nothing to fear;
I'll give you the best, both of welcome and cheer."

So the poor little fly, with a nod of his head,
  Bowed, smiled, and consented to do as he said;
And smacking his lips at the thought of the wine,
  Went up with the spider to rest and to dine.

Up a street and an alley of lilies and grass;
  Bees, butterflies, crickets start up as they pass,
And a small lady-bird ran to hide in a rose,
  For fear the great spider should tread on her toes.
To his mansion he came; it was knitted with thread,
  And built upon briers, with leaves overhead.
Without ringing the bell or tapping the door
  They enter at once on the back parlor floor;
And the fly, seizing hold of a king-cup of wine,
  When he'd swallowed it down, really thought it
    so fine
That a blue bottle full by his side on the floor
  He drained at a breath, and then asked for some
    more.

He drank the drink till he suddenly found
  That spider and king-cups were all turning round,
And, alarmed, he'd at once have been off like a shot,
  But he found that his feet were enchained to the
    spot,
"O good Mr. Spider! unfasten my feet,"
  Said the fly, "for I've a lady to meet;
Oh! don't look so fierce—I'm dizzy and queer.
  Pray, pray let me go! I've been long enough
    here."
'Twas all of no use, for the poor little fly
  Was killed by the spider to make up his pie—

A bee who was passing at twelve heard his groans,
And a cricket at night saw the ants at his bones.

There are men, like the spider, who " make up their
    pies "
By luring their fellows and blinding their eyes;
They tempt them with drink till they've come to dis-
    grace,
And fasten their feet, like the fly's, to the place.
They build up their webs, both in country and town,
    To catch high and low, from the lord to the clown;
There are inns for the rich, and shops for the poor,
    Full of wine, gin, and rum to attract and allure.
They'll perhaps talk to you of " their house full of
    wine,"
And tempt you with that to come in and dine;
But beware! and take care by the fate of the fly,
    For be sure they but want you to " make up their
    pie."

                JOHNSON BARKER.

TEMPERANCE.

SOME men look upon this temperance cause as
whining bigotry, narrow asceticism, or a vulgar
sentimentality, fit for little minds, weak women,
and weaker men. On the contrary, I regard it as
second only to one or two others of the primary
reforms of this age, and for this reason,—every race
has its peculiar temptation; every clime has its
specific sin. The tropics and tropical races are

tempted to one form of sensuality; the colder and temperate regions, and our Saxon blood, find their peculiar temptation in the stimulus of drink and food.

In old times, our heaven was a drunken revel. We relieve ourselves from the over-weariness of constant and exhausting toil by intoxication. Science has brought a cheap means of drunkenness within the reach of every individual. National prosperity and free institutions have put into the hands of almost every workman the means of being drunk for a week, on the labor of two or three hours. With that blood and that temptation, we have adopted democratic institutions, where the law has no sanctions but the purpose and virtue of the masses. The statute-book rests not on bayonets, as in Europe, but on the hearts of the people.

A drunken people can never be the basis of a free government. It is the corner-stone neither of virtue, prosperity, nor progress. To us, therefore, the title deeds of whose estates, and the safety of whose lives, depend upon the tranquillity of the streets, upon the virtue of the masses, the presence of any vice which brutalizes the average mass of mankind and tends to make it more readily the tool of intriguing and corrupt leaders, is necessarily a stab at the very life of the nation. Against such a vice is marshalled the temperance reformation.

That my sketch is no fancy picture, every one of you knows. Every one of you can glance back over your own path, and count many and many a one among those who started from the goal at your side, with equal energy, and perhaps greater promise, who has found a drunkard's grave long before this. The brightness of the bar, the ornament of the pulpit, the hope and blessing and stay of many a family—you know, every one of you who has reached middle life, how often on your path has been set up the warning, "Fallen before the temptations of the streets!" Hardly one house in this city, whether it be full and warm with all the luxury of wealth, or whether it find hard, cold maintenance by the most earnest economy, no matter which,—hardly a house that does not count among sons or nephews some victim of this vice. The skeleton of this warning sits at every board.

The whole world is kindred in this suffering. The country mother launches her boy with trembling upon the temptations of city life. The father trusts his daughter anxiously to the young man she has chosen, knowing what a wreck intoxication may make of the house-tree they set up. Alas! how often are their worst forebodings more than fulfilled! I have known a case—probably many of you recall some almost equal to it—where one worthy woman could count father, brother, husband and son-in-law, all drunkards, no man among her near kindred, except her son, who was not a victim of this vice. Like all other appetites, this finds resolution weak when set against the constant presence of temptation.

WENDELL PHILLIPS.

TOMMY BROWN.

"WHAT is your name?" asked the teacher.

"Tommy Brown, ma'am," answered the boy.

He was a pathetic little figure, with a thin face, large, hollow eyes and pale cheeks that plainly told of insufficient food. He wore a suit of clothes evidently made for some one else. They were patched in places with cloth of different colors. His shoes were old, his hair cut square in the neck in the unpracticed manner that women sometimes cut boys' hair. It was a bitter day, yet he wore no overcoat, and his bare hands were red with the cold.

"How old are you, Tommy?"

"Nine year old come next April. I've learnt to read at home, and I can cipher a little."

"Well, it is time for you to begin school. Why have you never come before?"

The boy fumbled with a cap in his hands, and did not reply at once. It was a ragged cap, with frayed edges, and the original color of the fabric no man could tell.

Presently he said: "I never went to school 'cause —'cause—well, mother takes in washin', an' she couldn't spare me. But sissy is big enough now to help, an' she minds the baby besides."

It was not quite time for school to begin. All around the teacher and the new scholar stood the boys that belonged in the room. While he was making his confused explanation some of the boys laughed, and one of them called out, "Say, Tommy, where are your cuffs and collar?" And another said, "You must sleep in the ragbag at night, by the looks of your clothes!" Before the teacher could quiet them, another boy had volunteered the information that the father of the new boy was "old Si Brown, who is always as drunk as a fiddler."

The poor child looked round at his tormentors like a hunted thing. Then, before the teacher could detain him, with a suppressed cry of misery he ran out of the room, out of the building, down the street, and was seen no more.

The teacher went to her duties with a troubled heart. All day long the child's pitiful face haunted her. At night it came to her dreams. She could not rid herself of the memory of it. After a little trouble, she found the place where he lived, and two of the W. C. T. U. women went to visit him.

It was a dilapidated house in a street near the river. The family lived in the back part of the house, in a frame addition. The ladies climbed the outside stairs that led up to the room occupied by the Brown family. When they first entered, they could scarcely discern objects, the room was so filled with the steam of the soapsuds. There were two windows, but a tall brick building adjacent shut out the light. It was a gloomy day, too, with gray, lowering clouds that forbade even the memory of sunshine.

A woman stood before a washtub. When they

entered, she wiped her hands on her apron and
came forward to meet them.

Once she had been pretty. But the color and
light had all gone out of her face, leaving only
sharpened outlines and haggardness of expression.

She asked them to sit down, in a listless, uninter-
ested manner; then, taking a chair herself, she
said :—

"Sissy, give me the baby."

A little girl came forward from a dark corner of
the room, carrying a baby, that she laid in its
mother's lap—a lean and sickly looking baby with
the same hollow eyes that little Tommy had.

" Your baby doesn't look strong," said one of the
ladies.

" No, ma'am ; she ain't very well. I have to
work hard and I expect it affects her;" and the
woman coughed, as she held the child to her
breast.

This room was the place where this family ate,
slept, and lived. There was no carpet on the floor ;
an old table, three or four chairs, a broken stove, a
bed in one corner; in an opposite corner a trundle-
bed—that was all.

" Where is your little boy, Tommy ?" asked one
of the visitors.

" He is there in the trundle-bed," replied the
mother.

" Is he sick ?"

" Yes'm, and the doctor thinks he ain't going to
get well." At this the mother laid her head on the

baby's face, while the tears ran down her thin and faded cheeks.

"What is the matter with him?"

"He was never very strong, and he's had to work too hard, carrying water and helping me lift the washtubs and things like that."

"Is his father dead?"

"No, he ain't dead. He used to be a good workman and we had a comfortable home. But all he earns now—and that ain't much—goes for drink. If he'd only let me have what little I make over the washtub. But half the time he takes that away from me, and then the children go hungry."

She took the child off her shoulder. It was asleep now, and she laid it across her lap.

"Tommy had been crazy to go to school. I never could spare him till this winter. He thought if he could get a little education, he'd be able to help take care of Sissy and baby and me. He knew he'd never be able to work hard. So I fixed up his clothes as well as I could, and last week he started. I was afraid the boys would laugh at him, but he thought he could stand it if they did. I stood in the door and watched him go. I can never forget how the little fellow looked," she continued, the tears streaming down her face. "His patched-up clothes, his old shoes, his ragged cap, his poor little anxious look. He turned around to see me as he left the yard, and said, 'Don't you worry, mother; I ain't going to mind what the boys say.' But he did mind. It wasn't an hour till he was back again.

I believe the child's heart was just broke. I
thought mine was broke years ago. If it was, it
was broke over again that day. I can stand most
anything myself, but oh, I can't bear to see my
children suffer!" Here she broke down in a fit of
convulsive weeping. The little girl came up to her
quietly and stole a thin little arm round her
mother's neck. "Don't cry, mother," she whispered, "don't cry."

The woman made an effort to check her tears,
and wiped her eyes. As soon as she could speak
with any degree of calmness, she continued:—

"Poor little Tommy cried all day; I couldn't
comfort him. He said it wasn't any use trying to
do anything. Folks would only laugh at him for
being a drunkard's little boy. I tried to comfort
him before my husband came home. I told him his
father would be mad if he saw him crying. But it
wasn't any use. Seemed like he couldn't stop.
His father came and saw him. He wouldn't have
done it if he hadn't been drinking. He ain't a bad
man when he is sober. I hate to tell it, but he
whipped Tommy. And the child fell and struck
his head. I suppose he'd 'a' been sick, any way.
But, oh, my poor little boy! My sick, suffering
child!" she cried. "How can they let men sell a
thing that makes the innocent suffer so?"

A little voice spoke from the bed. One of the
ladies went to him. There he lay, poor little
defenceless victim. He lived in a Christian land, in
a country that takes great care to pass laws to pro-

tect sheep and diligently legislates over its game. Would that the children were as precious as brutes and birds!

His face was flushed, and the hollowed eyes were bright. There was a long purple mark on his temple. He put one little wasted hand to cover it, while he said:—

"Father wouldn't have done it if he hadn't been drinking." Then, in his queer, piping voice, weak with sickness, he half whispered: "I'm glad I'm going to die. I'm too weak ever to help mother, anyhow. Up in heaven the angels ain't going to call me a drunkard's child, and make fun of my clothes. And maybe if I'm right there where God is, I can keep reminding him of mother, and he'll make it easier for her."

He turned his head feebly on his pillow, and then said, in a slower tone: "Some day—they ain't going—to let the saloons—keep open. But I'm afraid—poor father—will be dead—before then." Then he shut his eyes from weariness.

The next morning the sun shone in on the dead face of little Tommy.

He is only one of many. There are hundreds like him in tenement houses, slums and alleys in town and country. Poor little martyrs, whose tears fall almost unheeded; who are cold and hungry in this Christian land; whose hearts and bodies are bruised with unkindness! And yet "the liquor traffic is a legitimate business and must not be interfered with," so it is said.

Over eighteen hundred years ago, it was also said:—

"Whoso shall offend one of these little ones, it were better for him that a millstone were hanged about his neck, and that he were drowned in the depths of the sea."

COMMON SCHOOL EDUCATION.

THE VOICE OF DESPAIR.

BUT now the struggle is over, I can survey the field and measure the losses. I had position, high and holy. The demon tore from around me the robes of my sacred office, and sent me forth churchless and Godless—a very hissing and by-word among men. Afterward I had business, large and lucrative, and my voice in all large courts was heard pleading for justice, mercy, and right. But the dust gathered on my unopened books, and my foot-fall crossed the threshold of a drunkard's office. I had money ample for all necessities, but it took wings and went to feed the coffers of the devils which possessed me. I had a home adorned with all that wealth and the most exquisite taste could suggest. This devil crossed its threshold, and the light faded from its chambers; the fire went out on the holiest altars, and leading me through its portals, despair walked forth with her, and sorrow and anguish lingered within. I had children, beautiful, to me at least, as the dream of the morning, and they had so entwined themselves around their father's heart, that no matter where it might wander, ever it came back to them on the bright wings of a father's undying love. His destroyer took their hands in his and led them away. I had a wife whose charms of mind and person were such that to see her was to remember, and to know her was to love. . . .

For thirteen years we walked the rugged path of life together, rejoicing in its sunshine, and sorrowing in its shade. This infernal monster couldn't spare me even this. I had a mother, who for long, long years had not left her chair, a victim of suffering and disease, and her choicest delight was in the reflection that the lessons which she had taught at her knee had taken root in the heart of her youngest son, and that he was useful to his fellows, and an honor to her who bore him. But the thunderbolt reached even there, and there it did its most cruel work. Other days may cure all but this. Ah! me; never a word of reproach from her lips; only a tender caress; only a shadow of a great and unspoken grief gathering over the dear old face; only a trembling hand laid more lovingly on my head; only a closer clinging to the cross; only a more piteous appeal to heaven if her cup were not at last full. And while her boy raved in wild delirium two thousand miles away, the pitying angels pushed the golden gates ajar, and the mother of the drunkard entered into rest.

And thus I stand, a clergyman without a cure; a

barrister without a brief or business; a father without a child; a husband without a wife; a son without a parent; a man with scarcely a friend; a soul without a hope—all swallowed up in the maelstrom of drink.　　　　　　　　J. J. TALBOT.

COLD WATER.

THE thirsty flowerets droop; the parching grass
　　Doth crisp beneath the feet, and the wan trees
Perish for lack of moisture. By the side
Of the dried rills, the herds despairing stand,
With tongues protruded. Summer's fiery heat,
Exhaling, checks the thousand springs of life.

——Marked ye yon cloud glide forth on angel wing?
Heard ye the herald drops, with gentle force,
Stir the broad leaves? and the protracted rain,
Waking the streams to run their tuneful way?
Saw ye the flocks rejoice, and did ye fail
To thank the God of fountains?

　　　　　　　　See,—the hart
Pants for the water-brooks. The fervid sun
Of Asia glitters on his leafy lair,
As fearful of the lion's wrath, he hastes,
With timid footsteps, through the whispering reeds,
Quick leaping to the renovating stream;
The copious draught his bounding veins inspires
With joyous vigor.

Patient o'er the sand,
The burden-bearer of the desert clime,
The camel, toileth.   Faint with deadly thirst,
His writhing neck of bitter anguish speaks.
Lo ! an oasis, and a tree-girt well !—
And, moved by powerful instinct on he speeds,
With agonizing haste, to drink, or die.
On his swift courser, o'er the burning wild
The Arab cometh. From his eager eye
Flashes desire.   Seeks he the sparkling wine,
Giving its golden color to the cup?
No ! to the gushing stream he flies, and deep
Buries his scorching lip, and laves his brow,
And blesses Allah.

Christian pilgrim, come!
Thy brother of the Koran's broken creed
Shall teach thee wisdom, and with courteous hand,
Nature, thy mother, holds the crystal cup,
And bids thee pledge her in the element
Of temperance and health.

Drink and be whole,
And purge the fever poison from thy veins,
And pass, in purity and peace, to taste
The river flowing from the throne of God.

Mrs. Sigourney.

THE ORIGINAL LIQUOR LEAGUE.

ONE day the bad spirits met together and resolved that our human race were too happy,
and a delegation of four infernals were sent up to
earth on an embassy of mischief. One spirit said:
"I will take charge of the vineyards!" Another
said: "I will look after the grain-fields!" Another
said: "I will supervise the dairy!" Another said:
"I will take charge of the music!" They landed
in the great Sahara desert, clutched their skeleton
fingers in a handshake of fidelity, kissed each other
good-bye with lip of blue flame, and separated for
their mission.

The first spirit entered the vineyard one bright
morning, and sat down on the twisted root of a
grape-vine in sheer discouragement. He could not
at first plan any harm for the vineyard. The clusters were so full, and purple, and luscious, and pure.
The air was fairly bewitched with their sweetness;
health seemed to breathe from every ripened bunch.
But in wrath at so much loveliness, the fiend
grasped a cluster in his right hand, and squeezed it
with utter hate, and lo! his hand was red with the
liquid, and began to smoke. Then the fiend laughed
and said, as he looked at the crimson stream drip-
ping from his hand: "That makes me think of the
blood of broken hearts. I will strip the vineyard
and squeeze out all the clusters, and let the juices
stand till they rot, and will call the process 'fer-

mentation.'" And a great vat was made, and men, seeing it, brought cups and pitchers, and dipped them in, and went off, drinking as they went till they dropped in long lines of death, so that when the fiend of the vineyards wanted to go back to his home in the pit, he trod on the bodies of the slain all the way, going down over a causeway of the dead.

The fiend of the grain-field waded chin-deep through the barley and the rye. As he came in he found all the grain talking about bread, and prosperous husbandmen, and thrifty homes. But the fiend thrust his long arms through the barley and rye, and pulled them up and flung them into the water, and kindled fires beneath, by a spark from his own heart, and there was a grinding, and a mashing and a stench. And men dipped their bottles into the fiery juice, and staggered, and blasphemed, and rioted, and fought, and murdered, till the fiend of the grain-field was so well pleased with their behavior, he changed his residence from the pit to a whiskey-barrel; and there he sits by the doorway, at the bung-hole, laughing right merrily at the fact that out of so harmless a thing as barley and rye, he has made this world a suggestion of Pandemonium.

The fiend of the dairy met the cows as they were coming up full-uddered from the pasture-field. As the maid milked, he said: "It will not take me long to spoil that mess. I will add to it some brandy, and sugar, and nutmeg, and stir them into a milk punch, and children will like it, and even temperance men will take it; and if I can do no more, I will make their heads ache, and hand them gradually over to the more vigorous fiends of the satanic delegation." And then he danced a break-down on the shelf of the dairy, till all the shining row of milk-pans quaked.

The fiend of music entered a grog-shop and found the customers few. So he made a circuit of the city, and gathered up all the instruments of sweet sound, and after the night had fallen, he marshalled a band, and trombone blew, and cymbals clapped, and harp thrummed, and drum beat, and bugle called, and crowds thronged in and listened, and, with wine-cup in their right hand, began to whirl in a dance that grew wilder, and stronger, and rougher, till the room shook, and the glasses cracked, and the floor broke through, and the crowd dropped into hell.

They had done their work so well, these fiends of vineyard, and grain-field, and dairy, and concert-saloon, that, on getting back, high carnival was held, Satan from his throne announcing the fact that there was no danger of the earth's redemption so long as the vineyards, and orchards, and grain-fields, and music paid such a large tax to the diabol-ical. Then all the satyrs, and spirits, and demons cried "Hear! hear!" and, lifting their chalices of fire, drank "Long life to rumsellers! Prosperity to the gallows! Success to the liquor league."

Rev. T. De Witt Talmage.

RIGHT MAKES MIGHT.

THOUGH you see no banded army,
    Though you hear no cannon's rattle,
We are in a mighty contest,
    We are fighting a great battle.
      We are few, but we are right,
      And we wage the holy fight,
      Night and day, and day and night.

If we do not fail or falter,
    If we do not sleep or slumber,
We shall win in this great contest,
    Though the foe is twice our number.
      This the burden of our song—
      We are few, but we are strong,
      And right must triumph over wrong.

THE BUSINESS SIDE OF PROHIBITION.

IN getting evidence of improvement or deterioration in a city you must go to the working classes. Especially is this true of Atlanta, because this is the third city in the United States in the proportion of workers to population.

Now here is a class of people representing in the workers of our number 47 per cent. of the entire population. Add the women and children who do not work, and we see this class represents 66 or 70 per cent. of our population. If I have shown that this class is benefited in an unspeakable manner by the untried experiment of prohibition, is it not our duty to continue this experiment that the greatest good may come to the greatest number?

There is just one thing further. What harm has it done? If it has done harm, let us see what. They say we were going to be ruined, that bats and owls would fly in and out of our idle factories, and the real estate men have the renting of nine out of ten houses that are rented. They testify without a break, absolutely without a break, that they have fewer houses on their lists than they have ever had since they have been in business.

In the last two years there have been 687 citizens who have become home-owners, against 153 in the two years previous—citizens owing no man and owning no man as master, wearing the collar of no faction, free-born American citizens, not quibbling about personal liberty, but standing with wife and little ones, honest and independent, above penury and degradation.

I assume to keep no man's conscience; I assume to judge for no man; I do not assume that I am better than any man, but that I am weaker. But I say this to you, I have a boy as dear to me as the ruddy drops that gather about this heart. I find my hopes already centering in his little body, and I look to him to-night to take to himself the work that, strive as I may, must fall unfinished at last from my hands. Now, I tell you, if I were to vote to recall bar-rooms to this city, when I know that it has prospered in their absence, and that boy should fall through their agency, I tell you—and this conviction has come to me in the still watches of the night—I could not, wearing the crowning sorrow of his disgrace and looking into the eyes of her whose heart he had broken—I could not, if I had voted to recall these bar-rooms, find answer for my conscience or support for my remorse. I don't know how any other father feels, but that is the way I feel, if God permits me to utter the truth.

The best reforms of this earth come through waste and storm and doubt and suspicion; the sun itself when it rises on each day, wastes the radiance of the moon, and blots the starlight from the skies, but only to unlock the earth from the clasp of night and plant the stars anew in the opening flowers. Behind that sun as behind this movement we may be sure there stands the Lord God Almighty, master and maker of this universe, from whose hand the spheres are rolled to their orbits, and whose voice has been the harmony of this world since the morning stars sang together.

HENRY W. GRADY.

THINK BEFORE YOU DRINK.

HE who thinks before he drinks
    Will nothing drink but water,
He who drinks before he thinks
    Will drink what no one ought to.

THE DISENTHRALLED.

[Permission of Houghton, Mifflin & Co.]

HE had bowed down to drunkenness,
  An abject worshipper,
The pulse of manhood's pride had grown
  Too faint and cold to stir;
And he had given his spirit up
  Unto the evil thrall;
And, bowing to the poisoned cup,
  He gloried in his fall.

There came a change—the cloud rolled by
  And light fell on his brain,
And like the passing of a dream
  That cometh not again,
The shadow of his spirit fled;
  He saw the gulf before,
He shuddered at the waste behind,
  And was a man once more.

He shook the serpent folds away,
  That gathered round his heart,
As shakes the wind-swept forest oak
  Its poison vine apart;
He stood erect; returning pride
  Grew terrible within,
And conscience sat in judgment on
  His most familiar sin.

The light of intellect again
  Along his pathway shone,

And reason like a monarch sat
  Upon its olden throne;
The honored and the wise once more
  Within his presence came,
And lingered oft on lovely lips
  His once forbidden name.

There may be glory in the might
  That treadeth nations down—
Wreaths for the crimson warrior,
  Pride for the kingly crown;
But nobler is that triumph hour,
  The disenthralled shall find,
When evil passion boweth down,
  Unto the Godlike mind!

J. G. WHITTIER.

THE QUESTION OF NATIONS.

THE idea that alcohol is necessary to enable men to perform extra mental or physical work has so utterly come to grief, it is really not necessary that I should put it forward, even as a remnant of superstition against us; but it has been suggested, leaving the present ground of history altogether, giving up, in despair, all attempts to reply to those unanswerable modern proofs against the old fallacy, which Arctic explorers, men of great strength and physical skill, incessant minds, and the most laborious literary scholars so richly supply; it has been suggested, I repeat, that, in some inscrutable manner, alcohol has been the feeding-mother of great nations, that it has sustained racial tenacities and vitalities, overcome mighty adversaries, and been, in short, both a herald and a conqueror on the side of civilization. For our part we, who dare to doubt this conclusion, want to know on what facts the conclusion is based. We are willing to learn, but we insist that those who preach must prove. Who can say what any great and mighty nation would have been to-day if wine had never been? By what evidence can the destinies of nations in favor of a good destiny be traced through wine or strong drink? We can see some facts in history in relation to the effects of human acts plainly enough. We can see, for instance, that Constantine most probably destroyed the Roman empire by moving the seat of government from its old basis to a new city that should be marked by his name. But where is there any corresponding fact bearing on great events and making of nations, wine being the factor? Suppose we turn to some facts, such as they are, in history, and they point circumstantially all the other way. Nations the mightiest have risen while they were abstaining nations; have fallen when wine became their luxury. Herodotus gives us the record of all-powerful Cyrus receiving from a small Ethiopian prince a bow, with this message: "Tell Cyrus that when he can bend this bow, which is mine, or find a Persian to do it, he may come and conquer Macrobia." And the historian relates, with evident satisfaction, that these Macrobians, who were

the finest of men, so that they stood a head above
the Persians, and were a truly noble race, were distinguished from the Persians in that they drank no
fluid stronger than milk, while the Persians revelled
in wine. There is yet another bit of evidence
against a hypothesis of alcohol as the nursing-
mother of great nations. Through all tribulations,
through all vicissitudes, through all persecutions,
what nation has maintained its vitality like the Jew-
ish nation? Has alcohol been to this people a
nursing-mother? Baron Haller, dealing with this
topic in the last century, gave the secret of the
cause of this vitality all in one word—Sobrietas.

B. W. RICHARDSON, M. D.

THE DOWN GRADE.

THE way to destruction is pointed and clear;
   It starts with a longing for cider and beer.
It promises pleasure, enjoyment, and fun,
Four hogsheads, full measure, to every tun.

And as on the way you farther advance
You go for French brandy that never saw France,
Till you slide down the way of destruction with ease
And call for whatever decoction you please.

The chances are that if you walk in this way
You'll see many things that are sinful and gay,
And make the acquaintance, no doubt to your cost,
Of many whose hopes of redemption are lost.

Each step that is taken your heart will beguile,
For " Wine is a mocker," deceitful and vile;
It promises pleasure and fulness of joy,
And only has power to blight and destroy.

THOMAS R. THOMPSON.

LEAVE THE LIQUOR ALONE.

I'M anxious to tell you a bit of my mind,
    If it won't put you out of the way;
For I feel very certain you'll each of you find
    There's wisdom in what I would say.
We've maxims and morals enough and to spare,
    But I have got one of my own
That helps me to prosper and laugh at dull care;
    It's " Leave the liquor alone."
If you'd win success and escape distress,
    Leave the liquor alone.
To avoid neglect and to win respect
    Leave the liquor alone.

The brewer can ride in a coach and pair,
    The drinker must trudge on the road;
One gets through the world with a jaunty air,
    The other bends under a load.
The brewer gets all the beef, my lads,
    And the drinker picks the bone;
If you'd have your share of good things, take care
    And leave the liquor alone.

You'll enjoy good health, and you'll gain in wealth,
  If you leave the liquor alone.
A man full of malt isn't worth his salt;
  Leave the liquor alone.

A drinker is ready to own at last
  He played but a losing game;
How glad would he be to recall the past
  And earn him a nobler name!
Don't reach old age with this vain regret
  For a time that's past and gone;
You may win a good prize in life's lottery yet
  If you'll leave the liquor alone.
You find some day it's the safest way
  To leave the liquor alone.
Resolve like men not to touch again;
  Leave the liquor alone.

THE LIPS THAT TOUCH LIQUOR SHALL NEVER TOUCH MINE.

ALICE LEE stood awaiting her lover one night,
  Her cheeks flushed and glowing, her eyes full
    of light.
She had placed a sweet rose 'mid her wild flowing
    hair;
No flower of the forest e'er looked half so fair
As she did that night, as she stood by the door
Of the cot where she dwelt by the side of the moor.

Her lover had promised to take her a walk,
And she built all her hopes on a long, pleasant talk ;
But the daylight was falling, and also, I ween,
Her temper was fading, 'twas plain to be seen;
For now she'd stand still, then a tune she would
      hum,
And impatiently mutter, "I wish he would come!"

"You may say what you like, 'tis not pleasant to
      wait
And William has oft kept me waiting of late;
I know where he stays, 'tis easy to tell,
He spends many an hour at the sign of the Bell;
I wish he would keep from such places away,
His rakish companions do lead him astray.

She heard a quick step, and her young heart beat
      fast
As she said, "I am glad he is coming at last;"
But it was only a neighbor who hastened to speak,
And he marked the quick flush on the young maid-
      en's cheek
And his aged eye twinkled with pleasure and glee,
As he merrily said, "So you're waiting, I see.

"Now don't at all think I'm intending to blame,
For love ought ne'er be a subject of shame;
But I tell you to warn you. I fancy, my lass,
Young William is getting too fond of the glass!
And, oh! if you wish for the love that endures,
Say that the lips that touch liquor shall never touch
      yours."

He went on his way, but the truth he'd impressed
Took root and sank deep in the young maiden's
    breast,
And strange things she scarce could account for
    before
Now appeared quite plain, as she pondered them o'er.
She then said, with a look of deep sorrow and fright,
" I really believe that the old man is right.

" When William next comes I will soon let him know
He must give up the liquor, or else he must go;
'Twill be a good chance, no doubt, to prove
If he is really sincere in his vows of deep love;
He must give up at once and forever the wine,
For the lips that touch liquor shall never touch
    mine."

She heard a quick step coming over the moor,
And a merry voice which she had oft heard before,
And ere she could speak a strong arm held her fast,
And a manly voice whispered, "I've come, love, at
    last.
I'm sorry that I've kept you waiting like this,
But I know you'll forgive me, then give me a kiss."

But she shook her bright curls on her beautiful
    head,
And she drew herself up while quite proudly she
    said,
" Now, William, I'll prove if you really are true,
For you say that you love me—I don't think you do;

If really you love me you must give up the wine,
For the lips that touch liquor shall never touch
　　mine."

He looked quite amazed.　"Why, Alice, 'tis clear
You really are getting quite jealous, my dear."
"In that you are right," she replied; "for, you see,
You'll soon love the liquor far better than me.
I'm jealous, I own, of the poisonous wine,
For the lips that touch liquor shall never touch
　　mine."

He turned, then, quite angry, "Confound it!" he
　　said,
"What nonsense you've got in your dear little head;
But I'll see if I can not remove it from hence."
She said, "'Tis not nonsense, 'tis plain common-
　　sense:
And I mean what I say, and this you will find,
I don't often change when I've made up my mind."

He stood all irresolute, angry, perplexed:
She never before saw him look half so vexed;
But she said, "If he talks all his life I won't flinch;"
And he talked, but he never could move her an inch.
He then bitterly cried, with a look and a groan,
"O Alice, your heart is as hard as a stone."

But though her heart beat in his favor quite loud,
She still firmly kept to the vow she had vowed;
And at last, without even a tear or a sigh,
She said, "I am going, so, William, good-bye."

"Nay, stay," he then said, "I'll choose one of the
    two—
I'll give up the liquor in favor of you."

Now, William had often great cause to rejoice
For the hour he had made sweet Alice his choice;
And he blessed through the whole of a long, useful
    life,
The fate that had given him his dear little wife.
And she, by her firmness, won to us that night
One who in our cause is an ornament bright.

Oh! that each fair girl in our abstinence band
Would say: "I'll ne'er give my heart or my hand
Unto one who I ever had reason to think
Would taste one small drop of the vile, cursed
    drink;"
But say, when you are wooed, "I'm a foe to the wine,
And the lips that touch liquor shall never touch
    mine."

HARRIET A. GLAZEBROOK.

THE SALOON AND THE HOME.

BREAK down the American home, and the fabric
of free government goes down with it. There
is no fountain of influence so pure as the Christian
home. Corrupt that, and every artery of national life
will be tainted. There is no teacher of public morals
so potential as the Christian mother. Weaken her

influence, and by so much you imperil the integrity of the nation. There is no school of political morality compared to the Christian home. Lure the pupils from that school-room, and you are recruiting the ranks of the enemy. For its own safety this Government must build around its homes all possible safeguards, and by every means in its power protect these nurseries of her future statesmen and rulers.

What shall we do with this liquor evil? To that question the best thought of the commonwealth is turning to-day, and with that problem the clearest brain of the nation is grappling. We can not push that question aside if we would. And surely no earnest man would if he could. What, then, is the duty of the hour? Do you say, Yes, we will regulate this business. We will take it under control and hold it within proper bounds by license. Then, we say, we are not seeking that kind of alliance. We invoke the aid of the law against this traffic as a criminal and a law-breaker, an enemy and a destroyer, and your proposition to license does not meet that demand. Licensing does not diminish the results of intemperance, and that is the end we are seeking. Licensing legalizes, and makes respectable in the eye of the law, a business that is illegal and disreputable. Consenting to license, makes the consentor measurably responsible for the traffic and its horrible fruits.

Lord Chesterfield said in the English House of Lords, more than one hundred years ago:

"Luxury, my lords, is to be taxed, but vice prohibited, let the difficulty in the law be what it will. Would you lay a tax on a breach of the Ten Commandments? Would not such a tax be wicked and scandalous? Would it not imply an indulgence to all those who could pay the tax? Vice, my lords, is not properly to be taxed, but to be suppressed. Luxury, or that which is only pernicious by excess, though not strictly unlawful, may be made more difficult. But the use of those things which are simply hurtful in their own nature, and in every degree, is to be prohibited. None, my lords, ever heard, in any nation, of a tax upon adultery, because a tax implies a license granted for the use of that which is taxed, to all who are willing to pay for it. Drunkenness is universally and in all circumstances an evil, and, therefore, ought not to be taxed, but prohibited."

That was the sentiment of an English statesman uttered one hundred years ago, and we repeat it to-day. We ask that this iniquity shall be suppressed by law. It is not only the right, but the duty of the Government to interdict the manufacture and sale of this great crime-producer, for the protection of its own life, and to protect the life and property of its subjects.

Rev. E. K. Young.

A NATIONAL PROHIBITION PARTY OUR ONLY DELIVERER.

THE destiny of man is the concern of the world. God in creation made him the great central idea, and gracious Providence operates the world to-day for man's good.

What can we do for man? What does he need? Where is the great disturber of his peace, and in what form may we find him? If the philanthropy of the age may testify; if the Christianity of the world may answer; if criminal courts and insane asylums may bear record, it is the demon of drink as embodied in the liquor traffic in our own fair land. The manufacture and sale of intoxicating drink is the great overshadowing curse of modern civilization.

It is not only a crime in itself, but a crime producing crime, a crime multiplying crime. The source whence issues the germ of every crime known to the courts; the source whence comes the inspiration of any deed that may chance suggest itself to the whisky-crazed brain of the drunken debauchee. It is to-day rearing amid the happy homes of' this God-favored people a class of beings as low, and as vile, and as utterly sunken in the scale of being as are the Hottentots in the jungles of Africa.

Its ravages are everywhere, its withering blight on every good thing. It is of all business the most infernal; and the devils in darkness never devised an agency more destructive of man's well-being. In fact the prohibition of the liquor traffic would cure most of the evils that afflict our people. Reform here means reform elsewhere; reform here means the uplifting and the upbuilding of the masses of our people, and a general reform of the customs of the nation. "This is a consummation devoutly to be wished," especially in our corrupted politics, where more than elsewhere we see the power exerted by the liquor party through its alarming control of the votes of the country. In this field it is master of the situation and completely dominates both the Democratic and Republican parties. These parties seek office and the liquor party has power to confer office. The liquor party wants liquor legislation, and the office-holding politician can control legislation, hence mutual benefit suggests a political alliance, and that alliance exists and has for years, as the champions of temperance reform long ago learned, to their disappointment and chagrin. This alliance is the combination prohibition has to meet. It is not a foe to be trifled with. It is unscrupulous and its resources are vast.

But prohibition based on principle, broad and deep, grounded on the divine idea of right, is destined to vanquish such a foe, sooner or later.

We will never stay the reign of drunkenness but by reign of law. We will never command the law until we can command votes through a party of Prohibitionists strong enough to sever all connection with the old parties, and boldly confront these at the ballot-box with a party organization committed to the idea of prohibition of the manufacture and sale of intoxicating liquors in the United States.

National prohibition is the demand, nothing less will satisfy. Anything less is only driving in the outer picket posts of the enemy, while the stronghold is untouched, the citadel secure. Any victory outside the field of politics is, at best, but temporary. We must reach a grand political party in the nation—a party whose power can demand. This power to demand gives the liquor party liquor legislation.

The Democratic press says Prohibitionists and Democrats can't live in the same political party together. The Republican press says that Prohibitionists must be prohibited in the Republican party.

The Liquor party says our only salvation from the Prohibition party is to give our solid vote for one of the old political parties; our business is safe in the hands of either the Democrats or Republicans. Now, my friends, how can any Prohibitionist with such statements confronting him, hope for any aid to the Prohibition cause, from either of the old party organizations?

REV. DR. J. C. RAY.

ARREST ALCOHOL AND LIBERATE MAN.

WHAT has given the liquor traffic the power to get into the heart of the Christian republic, and rear its black death-flag by the side of our national flag, and to cut off in the United States alone one soul every eight minutes, and send it into eternity, under circumstances from which we are led to believe that they are excluded forever from Heaven, and from the glory of God?

What we license, we protect; what we license, we wrap the flag of the country around and make it a legitimate branch of business, and in the legalized aspect of the traffic lies its power. What does God's Word say about it? What does it say about licensed wrong? If Isaiah had seen the license system of the United States as it is now, he could not have better expressed it than he has, " Woe unto him that justifieth the wicked for a reward." The license system takes the money from these men who are dealing out liquid death for a government revenue, and thus makes it a legitimate branch of business, and God says, " Woe." I find every phrase of the subject of this work in the Bible. And I believe that God has wedded the Gospel and the temperance cause, and " what God hath joined together let no man put asunder." I find that the first prohibitory liquor-law ever passed was passed up in the Congress of Heaven, and it was not submitted to the people, it never had to be remodeled, and it never will be repealed, and then I found the awful iniquity of taking a revenue from the liquor traffic and putting it in the till of the government. "Woe to him that buildeth a town with blood and establisheth a city with iniquity."

Tax-payer, do you wonder why your taxes are so heavy? Go to the collector and ask him and he will tell you, "Don't you know we have had to increase the police force and put a wing on the county jail and enlarge the State's prison, and that we are about to build a new lunatic asylum? Seven-tenths of the lunacy of this country and England is the result of intemperance. The story of the good old Irish woman is a good lesson for us to learn. Her husband was frequently before the police court for committing offenses while under the influence of liquor, and she was in the habit of going before the magistrate who was to try him and begging him off, and this was her principal plea, that it was not Patrick that did it, but it was the whisky that was in him. "For," she said, "Patrick when sober was always a good man." But this time it was a more heinous crime he was up for, but she went before the judge and repeated the same thing over to him; but the judge would not hear of it, and he said to her, "It won't do any good to keep bothering us by repeating this over and over;" and finally she said to him, "I think it would be a good deal more sensible for yourself and the jury, if you would put the whisky in the penitentiary and let Patrick go to work."

PROHIBITION THE TRUE ANTI-POVERTY PARTY.

PROHIBITION is a grand and glorious fact. A protection to the home, a safeguard to the family, the surety of the State. It is an economic, political and social fact, the glory of the present and the hope of the future.

In Maine, Kansas and Iowa, it has made liquor-selling a disgrace. It has greatly modified the drinking habits of young men. It has greatly reduced the number of saloons. It has shut up the distilleries and breweries. It has largely reduced the amount of drunkenness. It has virtually relieved the community of tramps and vagrants. It has increased the demand for labor. It has greatly reduced the taxes. It has added largely to the value of all kinds of property. It has nearly emptied the jails, prisons, and poorhouses.

It has greatly reduced the amount of sickness. It has greatly reduced the number of railroad, steamboat, and other accidents. It has elevated the moral character of the people. It has largely diminished litigation. It has contributed to the attendance at churches. It has increased the attendance at the schools.

It has greatly increased savings-bank deposits and banking capital. It has reduced the criminal cases before the court over 50 per cent. and crime of all kinds, including murders and violence, have diminished more than 75 per cent. It has added greatly to the volume of trade, including the demand for wearing apparel, pianos, sewing-machines, carpets, furniture, etc., etc., also increasing railroad traffic. In fact, all branches of business have had a greatly increased prosperity, and the people have better security for their lives, homes and property.

The above positively, clearly and unanswerably prove that when prohibition of the liquor traffic becomes general in both State and Nation, drunkenness, poverty, and crime will be almost unknown in the community, and the promised glorious good time will have come for the country. May God speed the day, and each Christian and patriotic citizen demonstrate that he realizes his personal responsibility for its consummation, by using his vote and his political opportunities when and where the liquor traffic can be crushed out by prohibition.

In the face of all these wonderful facts are there any who still insist that prohibition is impracticable and visionary, the pet theory of cranks only?

W. JENNINGS DEMOREST.

BOYS—AND THE BOTTLE.

NOTHING from the pen of Dickens or Thackeray goes nearer to the fount of tears than many a scene in child-life which is occurring every day. Not long ago I came upon a staggering father who was being led home by his own little boy. When the helpless sot reeled over and was likely to fall, the lad dexterously steadied him up again, as if he had acquired the knack of it from a long experience. The expression of shame and grief on the poor child's face haunted me for hours. I shuddered to think that the accursed appetite might descend as an hereditary bane, and be reproduced in that child in future years. One of the most hopeless cases of drunkenness I ever knew was the case of a church-member whose father and grandfather were confirmed topers. That the lust for strong drink is hereditary has been often proved; but what father has a right to bequeath such a legacy of damnation to his offspring?

A few days ago an interesting lad called at my door with the request from his mother for me to visit her. "What is the matter, my lad?" His countenance clouded over as he said tearfully—"It's about papa." The old, old story. I knew it too well. "Papa" had broken loose again, and the seven evil spirits which had been cast out, had come back again, and the last state of the man became worse than before. Such visits are among the saddest which a pastor can ever be called to make; to me—after my long observation of the clutch which drunkenness fastens on its victim—they are among the most desperate. There is a bare possibility that the father may be saved; but what an example to his boy!

A friend gave me lately the experience of a skillful professional man in about the following words: "My early practice," said the doctor, "was successful, and I soon attained an enviable position. I married a lovely girl; two children were born to us, and my domestic happiness was complete. But I was invited often to social parties where wine was freely circulated, and I soon became a slave to its power. Before I was aware of it I was a drunkard. My noble wife never forsook me, never taunted me with a bitter word, never ceased to pray for my reformation. We became wretchedly poor, so that my family were pinched for daily bread.

"One beautiful Sabbath my wife went to church, and left me lying on a lounge, sleeping off my previous night's debauch. I was aroused by hearing something fall heavily on the floor. I opened my eyes and saw my little boy of six years old, tumbling upon the carpet. His older brother said to him— 'Now get up and fall again. That's the way papa does; let's play we are drunk!' I watched the child as he personated my beastly movements in a way that would have done credit to an actor! I arose and left the house, groaning in agony and remorse. I walked off miles into the country—thinking over my abominable sin and the example I was setting before my children. I solemnly resolved that with God's help I would quit my cups, and I did. No lecture I ever heard from Mr. Gough moved my soul like the spectacle of my own sweet boys 'playing drunk as papa does.' I never pass a day without thanking my God for giving me a praying wife, and bestowing grace sufficient to conquer my detestable sin of the bottle. Madam, if you have a son, keep him, if you can, from ever touching a glass of wine."

It is the ready excuse of many a young lad for taking a glass of champagne—"We always have it at home." The decanter at home kindles the appetite which soon seeks the drinking-saloon. The thoughtless or reckless parent gives the fatal push which sends the boy to destruction.

Long labor in the temperance reform has convinced me that the most effectual place to promote it is at home. There is the spot where the mischief too often is done. There is the spot to enact a "prohibitory law." Let it be written upon the walls of every house—Wherever there is a boy, there should never be a bottle.

REV. T. L. CUYLER, D. D.

THE DEMERITS OF HIGH LICENSE.

HIGH license puts no restriction upon the buyer. He can get his liquor, if he wishes it, just as copiously as before. One saloon will supply the craving of 500—or 5,000 for that matter—as well as many. The evils of intemperance are not, therefore, necessarily reduced by restricting the number of the saloons. Their abolition rather than their reduction is what we need and ought to seek.

License, high or low, takes away what ought to be an important moral restriction from the seller. It removes from him the condemnation of the com-

munity, and justifies him.   It makes his acts legal.
His moral sense, easily blinded by the enormous
profits of his trade, is thus paralyzed.   He becomes
thus what we find him to be, obdurate, rapacious,
an evil man and seducer, who waxes worse and worse.
I do not wish to condemn him or any man, but I
do not believe there is any trade so demoralizing to
the trader, any class of sales which does the seller
so much moral mischief, as that in intoxicating
drinks.   And to this damage the community con-
tributes by licensing his trade.

The moral tone of the community is lowered by
licensing the liquor traffic.   Whether it is right or
wrong *per se* to buy or sell or drink intoxicating
liquors, is a question I do not care to argue.   This
question loses its interest to me in the face of the
appalling facts with which the liquor traffic confronts us.   There is no single channel through
which such depths of misery flow over the human
race as through this.   No ravages of disease, no
devastations of nature, no kinds of vice or crime,
work such woe as this.   Such a statement no intelligent person will be likely to doubt, and no
honest man will deny.   Now, to license the liquor
traffic on the view that the enormity of this evil can
be regulated—impossible as experience has thus far
shown this to be—to sanction the opening of these
flood-gates on the pretense that to keep them shut
is to infringe upon the liberty which a wise government should ever guard, is not only, as it seems to
me, the enslavement of the multitude for the free-

dom of the few—an attempt whose result is likely
to be the bondage of all—but it makes the community itself a party to wrong doing. This cannot
be done without lowering its own moral tone.

The revenue from license falls heaviest where the
burden ought to be the least. The cost of the
license, while it may add to the price of the liquor
sold, does not, as far as I can learn, diminish the
amount of liquor bought and consumed. Practically, the cost of liquor within the limits which any
license is likely to put, seems to have little to do with
the consumption. An intemperate man is not likely
to drink more because it is cheap, or less because it
is dear. The difference between three cents a glass
and four, makes no appreciable difference with him.
But the family of the drunkard! Alas! alas! the
great revenues for high license, the enormous taxes
on intoxicating drinks, are wrung from the wretchedness of worse than widowed wives, and worse than
orphaned children!

PRESIDENT SEELYE.

THE DREAM OF THE REVELLER.

AROUND the board the guests were met, the
lights above them gleaming,
And in their cups, replenished oft, the ruddy wine
was streaming;
Their cheeks were flushed, their eyes were bright,
their hearts with pleasure bounded,

The song was sung, the toast was given, and loud
    the revel sounded.
I drained my bumper with the rest, and cried,
    "Away with sorrow;
Let me be happy for to-day, and care not for to-
    morrow!"
But as I spoke my sight grew dim, and slumber
    deep came o'er me,
And 'mid the whirl of mingling tongues, this vision
    passed before me:

Methought I saw a demon rise; he held a mighty
    beaker,
Whose burnished sides ran daily o'er with floods of
    burning liquor;
Around him pressed a clam'rous crowd, to taste this
    liquor greedy,
But chiefly came the poor and sad, the suff'ring and
    the needy;
All those oppressed by grief and debt, the dissolute
    and lazy,
Blear-eyed old men, and reckless youths, and palsied
    women crazy.
"Give, give!" they cry. "Give, give us drink to
    drown all thoughts of sorrow,
If we are happy for to-day, we care not for to-
    morrow!"

The first drop warms their shivering skins, and
    drives away their sadness;
The second lights their sunken eyes, and fills their
    souls with gladness;

The third drop makes them shout and roar, and
    play each furious antic;
The fourth drop boils their very blood, and the
    fifth drop drives them frantic.
"Drink!" says the demon, "drink your fill!
    Drink of these waters mellow,
They'll make your bright eyes blear and dull, and
    turn you white skins yellow;
They'll fill your home with care and grief, and
    clothe your back with tatters;
They'll fill your heart with evil thoughts—but never
    mind—what matters?

"Though virtue sink, and reasoning fail, and social
    ties dissever,
I'll be your friend in hour of need, and find you
    homes forever;
For I have built three mansions high, three strong
    and goodly houses—
A workhouse for the jolly soul who all his life
    carouses;
A hospital to lodge the sot, oppressed by pain and
    anguish;
A prison full of dungeons deep, where hopeless
    felons languish.
So drain the cup and drain again, and drown all
    thought of sorrow,
Be happy if you can to-day, and never mind to-
    morrow!"

But well he knows, this demon old, how vain is all
    his preaching;

The ragged crew that round him flock are heedless
    of his teaching;
Even as they hear his fearful words, they cry with
    shouts of laughter,
"Out on the fool! who mars to-day with thoughts
    of an hereafter!
We care not for thy houses three, we live but for
    the present,
And merry will we make it yet, and quaff our
    bumpers pleasant!"
Loud laughs the fiend to hear them speak, and lifts
    his brimming beaker,
"Body and soul are mine!" quoth he; "I'll have
    them both for liquor!"

CHARLES MACKAY.

PROHIBITION A BLESSING TO THE POOR.

WHEN you go to get the effect of a new movement for good or evil, where do you go? Not to the rich and idle, because you may swell or diminish their income and yet not change their habits; you simply diminish the hidden surplus. Nor to the middle class, because when you diminish their income they simply pinch themselves and pinch so quietly that their neighbors do not know it, or swell their incomes and they loosen out a little and pass something up to surplus. You cannot tell it there;

but go to the poorer classes—the men who labor for
their daily bread, and whose wages barely suffice to
give it to them; and there you find the first signs of
a good or evil movement. It is at once the truth
and reproach of our civilization, that starvation follows so close on labor that an evil movement is de-
tected in the hollow cheeks of little children and
the haggard faces of women before it is made manifest to the higher classes.

Mr. Geo. Adair rents houses to 1,300 tenants.
He states that he has issued in the last year one distress warrant where he issued twenty, two years ago.

I claim to be an intelligent man with some courage of conviction; but I pledge you my word, if that
one fact were established to my satisfaction, I
would vote for this thing if I never heard another
word on this subject. Have you thought what that
means—a distress warrant? It means eviction; it
means the very thing that is to-day kindling the
heart of this world for poor Ireland. It means
eviction! It means turning woman and her little
children out of the home that covers them, and to
which they are entitled. Mr. Tally, who rents 600
or 800 houses, says: "I used to issue two or three
distress warrants—four or five—a month. I have
not issued a single one in eighteen months." Now,
both of them are Prohibitionists. Harry Krouse
was an anti-Prohibitionist. He said: "My distress
warrants averaged thirty-six to the year, and I have
not issued one in twelve months."

I went down to Mr. Scott, who did not vote for

prohibition, and asked him. He said: "I have issued as many as twenty-five distress warrants in a month, and I have issued six in the last eighteen months, and five were to get people out of houses because they were obnoxious to their neighbors. I have issued one single distress warrant for failure to pay rent."

Is there any possible answer to that? Is there any industrial, any social, any economic revolution that has been worked since the world began that would account for the diminution in this most vicious and intolerable of legal enactments? Have you thought about what a distress warrant is?

Have you ever thought about a woman being turned out of her house—the little cottage that covers her and her children? Can you picture—you who live in comfortable homes filled with light and warmth and books and joy—can you think of these people—human beings, our brothers and sisters—the poor mother, brave, though her heart is breaking, huddling her little children about her—and the father, weak but loving, and loving all the deeper because he knows his weakness has brought them to this want and degradation—and little children, those of whom our Saviour said: "Suffer them to come unto me and forbid them not," there asking, "Mamma, where will we sleep to-night?"—can you picture that and then their taking themselves up and the woman putting her hand with undying love and faith in the hand of the man she swore to follow through good and evil report, and marching up

and down the street—this pitiable procession—
through the unthinking streets, by laughing children and shining windows, looking for a hole where,
like the foxes, they may hide their poor heads?

My friends, they talk to you about personal liberty, that a man should have the right to go into a
grog-shop and see this pitiable procession—now
stopped—parading up and down our streets again.
They talk to you about the shades of Washington,
Monroe and Jefferson. I would not give one happy,
rosy little woman, uplifted from that degradation—
happy again in her home, with the cricket chirping
on her hearthstone and her children about her knee,
her husband redeemed from drink at her side—I
would not give one of them for all the shades of all
the men that ever contended since Catiline con-
spired and Cæsar fought!

HENRY W. GRADY.

COULD I HAVE BORNE IT?

COULD I have borne it? I often think,
   If one of my idols had bowed to drink,
If one of my kings had laid his crown
At the feet of the mighty monster down;
If one of my darlings had sold his soul
For the pottage mess in a drunkard's bowl.

I thank Thee, dear Father, I do not know,
I thank Thee Thou hast not tried me so.

Could I have borne it? to see the light
Of the demon flash from the blue eyes bright,
Telling that reason and will had flown,
And wine and wildness sat on their throne.
While the sweet, pure look had gone from the face,
And base brutality sat in its place.
I thank Thee, dear Father, I do not know,
I thank Thee Thou hast not tried me so.

Could I have borne it? and live long years
With sorrow for meat, and drink of tears,
While the heart was dying of hunger and pain,
As it loved and longed and hoped in vain.
Oh! the dead that live on this bright glad day,
While the sunshine sweet o'er graves doth play.
I thank Thee, dear Father, I do not know,
I thank Thee Thou hast not tried me so.

If the plants I have loved, my own dear boys,
My care and my pride, my dearest joys,
If on them had fallen this dew of death,
And they never had wakened at morning's breath,
Would the spring for me have brought its flowers,
Or the roses have bloomed in summer bowers?
I thank Thee, dear Father, I do not know,
I thank Thee Thou hast not tried me so.

How many must bear it; the very air
Is full of the smoke of dwellings fair,

And the sound of sighing on every breeze,
While thousands are planting their willow-trees.
If the fire that lives in the fruit of the vine
Had scorched and blackened this home of mine,
How I could have borne it I do not know,
I thank Thee Thou hast not tried me so.

How many must bear it, the mighty woe
That is making graves o'er the hillsides grow,
That is tying the crape folds on cottage door,
And stilling the music on palace floor,
That is toppling the tallest towers down
Where the hands the hopes of men doth crown.
If it had come and called for my dead
And laid them to sleep in a hopeless bed.

Oh! it is better to praise than pray,
To be thankful than weep on this bright, glad day.
Help me to remember those who bear
An aching heart under garments fair;
Help me remember the tempted and tried;
Ever, good angels, be by their side.
Help me remember those who know,
And thank Thee Thou hast not tried me so.

MAY E. DUSTIN.

PROHIBITION THE ONLY SAFEGUARD FOR YOUTH.

WE mourn, as philanthropists and Christians, over the frightful perversion of so many young men, especially clerks and apprentices, in our larger cities; and we labor to save them through the church, the Sunday-school, and the Young Men's Christian Association. And all the while we are licensing a score of rum-shops along all the streets leading to every one of these fountains of life. On the South African plains vast herds of the hartbeest, the gemsbock, and other great antelopes pasture. They feed on the plains in the morning, and, when parched with the burning thirst of noon, they charge frantically, in rushing thousands, for the banks of the nearest river. But on their way a doom more terrible than thirst awaits them. Every devourer of the forest lurks for their coming. As they enter the jungle skirting the river, the ferocious tiger springs upon them. The lion, with his awful roar, dashes down among them from the shady rock. The spotted leopard bathes his jaws in their blood, and the great boa shoots his crushing coils from the overhanging tree, and enfolds them in his deadly embrace. Thus they perish every year by thousands, and their hungry foes riot and fatten on their blood. How frightfully true is all this, as a picture of the perils that surround the troops and hundreds of our young men and women in our cities. And the cruelest and direst devourer of all, the lord and leader of all the blood-lapping train, is the licensed rum-shop. It is our sacred duty to warn and admonish these unwary souls, to save and rescue all we can from destruction, and to bind up and heal the wounded and the torn. But all this, alone, will be of little avail. It is, indeed, salvation by retail; but what we want is salvation by wholesale! The devil devours by wholesale. Why, indeed, should we not save in the same way? We want to clear up that jungle! We want a grand hunt along that river! We want the magazine rifle and the explosive bullet to do their unerring work upon that army of bloody devourers! We want a wide and safe path opened for the innocent and panting herd to approach the waters of life! And this is just what we want in the temperance cause. We want the rum-shop driven from our streets. We want the rum demon, with all his grisly, impish crew, driven from our land forever. We want the law on the side of the victim, not against him. We want the jaw-teeth of the oppressor broken. We want the wide and safe highway of total prohibition cast up, that the "ransomed of the Lord," the souls for whom Christ died, may be first sobered and then converted, and so "return and come to Zion with songs and everlasting joy upon their heads!" We want "the powers that be" to be in truth "ordained by God" and not by the devil.

GEO. LANSING TAYLOR, D. D.

NATIONAL PROHIBITION.

NO party has ever risen into power so rapidly as the Prohibition party is now rising. The Anti-Slavery party came out from under the mountain of scorn and contempt to take the Presidential chair and both Houses of Congress; but the Prohibition party, if you will watch the statistics, is coming with four times the celerity. American slavery was a pet lamb as compared with this red dragon. All the families which have been robbed of fathers, brothers and sons by the rum traffic; and all the States of the Union that have been despoiled of their mightiest men; all the churches of Jesus Christ which find the chief obstacle to the advancement of religion in the appetite for strong drink; and all the intelligence, and all the patriotism, and all the enthusiasm of the land will yet pack itself into an avalanche that will come crushing down upon this, the worst evil that ever afflicted a nation. I give fair notice to all politicians in America of what is coming. Better lead off than follow in afterward as stragglers. Many of the strongest men in both political parties, North and South, see the rising tide of this reformation, and they are preparing to fight the red dragon. There may be many defeats before we get the final victory, but victory will come as surely as there is a God in heaven, for this nation was not intended for one great drunkery.

Oh! what a country this would be with no dram-shops! Then no poor-houses, no penitentiaries, fewer broken hearts and fewer disconsolate homes. No woman brought up in luxury, afterward married to a man who sets her, with her shriveled arm and hollow eye and pallid cheek and consuming lung, to fight back the wolf that thrusts its nostrils through the broken window-pane, snuffing for the blood of her helpless babe. Let the contention between the great temperance societies of America cease, and the 70,000 men belonging to the temperance societies of the State of New York join hands with the hundreds of thousands of temperance men in other States, and the millions of men who belong to no temperance society, but who are anxious for the sobriety and the disenthrallment of this country, and the work will be done, and done in less time than I tell you.

First of all, we want an amendment to the Constitution of the United States ratified by three-fourths of the States—an amendment prohibiting the manufacture and the sale of alcoholic liquors in all the States and Territories, except for medicinal, artistic, mechanical, and scientific purposes, and a prohibition of the importation of foreign alcoholic liquors except for the same purposes.

The mere prohibition of the manufacture and the sale of intoxicating liquors in a State, perhaps, may only drive that intoxication and that alcoholic liquor into another State; but let us have national prohibition, and then one-half the iniquity tumbles off into the Atlantic Ocean and the other half of the iniquity tumbles off into the Pacific Ocean—drowned in two oceans of cold water.

We want a national movement, so that the stronger States in the matter can help the weaker States, and so that the country districts can help the dissipated cities. We want a national movement.

Good citizens of America, I do not know how you feel, but I confess that I am tired of paying taxes to fix up the work of these infernal grog-shops that are tossing tens of thousands of people into crime and suffering. Out with them from Brooklyn! Out with them from the United States! I now proclaim war for the rest of my life against that abomination. State prohibition. National prohibition.

The work can be done, and it will be done; but it will not be done until the whole nation wakes up. State prohibition will not accomplish it. It must be national prohibition. You say, "Who would join such a party?" I will tell you. In the first place, hundreds of thousands of drunkards who, unable to endure the temptation, wish that these allurements were taken out of their sight. These poor tempted men cannot run the gauntlet of the bar-rooms and the wine-cellars. From morning until night they cannot get out of the way of these fascinations which are before them, behind them, on either side of them, an all-encircling fire of demoniac bombardment. Give these men a chance, and make it possible for them to walk the whole length of Fulton Street, Atlantic Street and Broadway, and Lasalle

Street, and Chestnut Street, and Pennsylvania Avenue, without the inhalation of alcoholic malodors.

Yea, all the patriots in both parties will come forth,the men who are tired of building asylums and penitentiaries and poor-houses, the men who want nothing themselves, but who want to have the land saved from drunkenness and crime, and to become a paradise for comfort and prosperity—domestic, social, national. For the Church of God, for all patriots, for all good women as well as all good men, let the battle cry for the next twenty-five years be, "Down with the rum traffic! National prohibition! No quarter for the license system! Eternal smash for the wine bottles! Death to the red dragon!"

                    T. De Witt Talmage, D. D.

GOD'S WORK.

GATHERING brands from the burning,
   Plucking them out of the fire.
Lifting the sheep that have wandered
   Out of the dust and the mire:
Bringing home sheaves from the harvest,
   To lay at the Master's feet—
Lord, all thy hosts of angels
   Must smile on a life so sweet.

Speaking with fear of no man,
   Speaking with love for all,
Warning the young and thoughtless
   From the wild beast, "Alcohol;"

Showing the snares that the tempter
　　Weaveth on every hand—
Lord, all thy dear, dear angels
　　Must smile on a life so grand.

Fighting the bloodless battle
　　With a heart that is true and bold—
Fighting it not for glory,
　　Fighting it not for gold,
But out of love for his neighbor,
　　And out of love for his Lord;
I know that the hands of the angels
　　Will crown him with his reward.

For whoso works for the Master,
　　And whoso fights His fight,
The angel's crown with a star-wreath;
　　And it glows with gems most bright.
They wear them for ever and ever,
　　The saints in that land of bliss,
And I know that heaven's best jewel
　　Is kept for a soul like this.

ELLA WHEELER WILCOX.

THE CLOSING SCENE.

ON the liquor vender stern Death had called,
　　He his last day on earth had passed;
The sins of the flesh and the love of gain,
　　Found a fitting rebuke at last.

His cold corpse lay in its damp bed of clay,
  And his salesrooms with crape were hung,
While he, himself, the spiritual man,
  To the cold river Styx had come.

Oh! the waves of that cruel stream flowed fast,
  He fain would have stayed on the land,
For the loose sails shook in the cutting blast,
  As he felt the force of Death's hand.
He entered the time-worn and dismal craft
  And trembled so in affright
That the weird and hideous boatman laughed
  Till the echoes darkened the night.

" Oh, where are we going?" the dealer cried.
  In mocking, sepulchral tone,
The ferryman Charon grimly replied:
  " To the gates of your future home."
A fearful voyage was that, in all truth,
  To the wretched and abject man;
His thoughts returned to the days of his youth,
  And he wished he was young again.

The boat touched the strand of a dreary land,
  " We separate here," Charon said;
On the shore stood Nemesis, pointing where
  A path through a dark tunnel led.
Impelled by a power he could not see,
  He followed his merciless guide
Until they arrived at a loathsome den,
  By the foot of a mountain side.

"Spirit," the regal custodian said,
"Behold here the home you have won!
Here you must live till your victims forgive
The numerous wrongs you have done.
The growth of seeds sown in your earthly home
You are called upon here to reap,
And here you must learn what you should have
known
Ere you planted those seeds so deep."

Grim dragons leered at the unhappy wretch,
Noisome serpents hissed in'the gloom,
As the ghastly guide turned the grating key
And left him alone to his doom.
Ah! who could find words for the thoughts that
flowed
Through the mind of the guilty man;
He cursed his fate through his chattering teeth,
And he wished he was young again.

Who are my accusers? Come, bring them to me,
My business was sanctioned by law,
I paid for a license," he hoarsely cried.
Oh! a terrible sight he saw,
For the first to come was a tiny child,
With a face that was pale and thin;
She slowly lifted a skeleton hand
And pointed it straight toward him :

" I have sobbed with hunger many a night,
As I lay on my bed of straw,
While my father paid you the price of bread—
Is starvation sanctioned by law ?

Before the bars of the damp prison doors
    A poor drunkard's wife next appeared;
He remembered well how, many a time,
    At her prayers and sobs he had sneered:

" I begged of you through my fast-falling tears,
    As I knelt on your bar-room floor,
Not to give to my half-crazed husband, rum,
    And at my petitions you swore.
My husband was killed in a drunken brawl,
    Brought on by the liquor you sold,
May you now drink of the bitterest draught
    That the depths of Hades can hold!"

A fair, blue-eyed boy, with a crimson gash
    Cut deep in the broad youthful brow,
And his murderer passed, with fearful oaths,
    By the door of the culprit now.
Full many a drunkard, with blood-shot eyes,
    And delirious, woeful form,
Lingered near, to mock him, with jeering cries,
    Ere the sad procession moved on.

There were little children, crying for bread,
    And mothers who wept for their sons,
And maidens, whose lovers to crime were led,
    Slowly greeted him. one by one.
Blind babes, deaf mutes, and children deformed
    In many a horrible way,
Their sentence passed on the penitent wretch
    During that, his settlement day.

Vainly he prayed in those hours for relief,
    For the past he could not efface,
And he tore his hair in remorseful grief,
    As the fruits of his sins he faced.
No license could help him under the weight
    Of the punishment he had won;
No arguments fair were efficient there,
    For his work could not be undone.

Oh! 'tis sad to think how many to-day,
    Sow seeds for harvest of tears,
And that they must reap at some future date
    The results of their wasted years.
They, too, must pass over the river Styx,
    With Charon, the ferryman old,
And Nemesis follows, to find their home
    But a cell in a mountain cold,—

A mountain whose walls are rocks of remorse
    That form round the spirit a cell,
Where serpents of pain and dragons of grief
    Are symbolized inmates of hell.
Oh, pause, ere too late, beware of your fate,
    Beware how you traffic with blood!
The curse of the lost is the certain cost
    To those who embark on its flood.

THE SURRENDER.

'TWAS a widow's home and a winter night;
    With moonlight and snow the world was white,
And out of the window a woman's eyes
Looked over the field and up at the skies

With a gaze that burned with a solemn ire
That leaped like a flame from a heart on fire.

Away and over the field of snow
They had carried her husband a month ago
To a drunkard's grave—and a drunkard's fame
Like the blight of the mildew had covered his name,
And her only son, with his father's thirst,
Like a fiend at his throat, by the demon cursed,
Was led in chains to the loathsome den
Where demons are made of the hearts of men.

She had plead with them, she had plead with him,
Till her cheek grew pale and her eyes grew dim;
She had pointed the way that his father trod
That led to that grave 'neath the frozen sod.
She had warned and counselled and prayed in vain—
His soul was held as by hook and chain;
And the demon laughed with chuckle and grin:
" Aha! " he said, " but I shall win!
Let the mother weep and beg and pine!
By the law of the land the right is mine.
There is no law like that of gold;
I have bought the right to win and hold.
I bought the right, and I bought it dear;
Shall I give it up for a woman's tear?"

Have I come to you with a story old
That is hackneyed and worn till it will not hold
To be passed around?   It is not new;
It is old as the crime that made it torn.
It has run through long chapters of grief and shame,
It has published its heroes name by name,

And how much they could drink as the standard of
    fame.
It has taken us down to the churchyard glooms,
And painfully led us among the tombs;
Then backward again to the shame and grief—
The same thing over as leaf by leaf.
The world has read it again and again
Till its heart grew numb to the sense of pain,
Till the eyes grow drowsy that used to weep;
And the tale went on, but the world was asleep.

But there is a change, and the story true
Is growing apace into something new.
The world is awake, and its ear is set,
Its lips are apart, and its eyelids wet;
For that night, while her boy was in the den
Where demons are made of the hearts of men,
While they filled the bowl that he quickly quaffed,
While they spake his mother's name, and laughed,
She out of her window, in stern despair,
Lifted to God a mother's prayer;
And God drew near her, and He laid His hand
Upon her with a strange command:
" Arise thou, therefore," said the Lord;
" Be doing, and you have my word:
Lo, I am with thee, and My power
Shall be thy heritage and dower."

" What can I do but weep?" she said.
" The work is great; send Thou instead
Some mighty one, for I am weak;
From out these tears how can I speak?"

Then came the word, "Canst thou refuse?
The weak things of the world I choose.
Nothing but love can conquer death;
Sin yields to none but trusting .Faith.
Take but thy broken heart of love;
The faith whose eye is turned above.
Go in thy weakness, and the strength
Of God shall be revealed at length."

Across the snow-clad field she went,
Her form beneath her burden bent:
Her shrinking steps despised the way
That to the haunt of demons lay,
The path whose end she knew too well—
The path whose steps take hold on hell.

She gained the door, she entered in:
The air was like the breath of sin;
But silence fell upon the throng,
The singer's voice dropped from his song,
Her son looked up with sullen eye.
She stood a moment silently,

Then silently she knelt and prayed;
They looked upon her, and, dismayed,
They felt the prayer they did not hear,
And trembled with a nameless fear.

She only prayed and turned away,
And took the path that homeward lay,
While in her inmost soul she felt
That God spake for her while she knelt.

Next day she went and knelt the same;
Without a word she went and came,
And day by day, with tearful face
And silent lips, she sought the place,
And poured the anguish of her prayer
Before the Lord, and left it there.

The place grew dreadful; for the Lord
In faithfulness fulfilled His word.
She went in weakness, but the strength
Of God was manifest; at length
His heavy hand upon them fell
And from the wine-cup swept the spell,
And in his soul the drinker shrank
E'en while the venomed cup he drank.

They watched for her; and when she came
They crept away with guilty shame;
And all day long, and all the night,
Asleep, awake, by dark or light,
That woman, with the silvery hair,
Just as she bowed in silent prayer,
Haunted the man who kept the den
Where demons were made of the hearts of men.

At length, one day, as the door she swung,
He met her, and asked, with faltering tongue,
How long she intended to come and pray?
" As long as you sell!"   He turned away
To hide from her his burning cheek,
To gather the voice with which to speak.
" Then I surrender!   I can not bear
This awful spell of a woman's prayer!"

So the den was closed, and bells were rung,
And shouts leaped forth, and songs were sung;
And like rushing flames the tidings flew
Of what a woman's prayer could do.

Then out of heaven there came a word,
And it filled and thrilled the hearts that heard:
" This work has waited a hundred years
For woman's prayer and woman's tears."

MRS. S. M. I. HENRY.

RUM THE WORST ENEMY OF THE WORK-ING-CLASSES.

GATHER up the money that the working-classes
have spent for rum during the last thirty years,
and I will build for every workingman a house, and
lay out for him a garden and clothe his sons in
broadcloth and his daughters in silks, and stand at
his front door a prancing span of sorrels or bays,
and secure him a policy of life insurance so that
the present home may be well maintained after he
is dead. The most persistent, most overpowering
enemy of the working-classes is intoxicating liquor.
It is the anarchist of the centuries, and has boy-
cotted and is now boycotting the body and mind
and soul of American labor. It is to it a worse foe
than monopoly, and worse than associated capital.
It annually swindles industry out of a large percent-
age of its earnings.

I will undertake to say that there is not a healthy laborer in the United States who, within the next twenty years, if he will refuse all intoxicating beverages and be saving, may not become a capitalist on a small scale.

But, oh, workingmen of America, take your morning dram, and your noon dram, and your evening dram, and spend everything you have over for tobacco and excursions, and you insure poverty for yourself and your children forever. If by some generous fiat of the capitalists of this country, or by a new law of the government of the United States, 25 per cent., or 50 per cent., or 100 per cent. were added to the wages of the working-classes of America, it would be no advantage to hundreds of thousands of them unless they stopped strong drink. Aye, until they quit that evil habit, the more money, the more ruin; the more wages, the more holes in the bag.

God only knows what the drunkard suffers. Pain files on every nerve, and travels every muscle, and gnaws every bone, and burns with every flame, and stings with every poison, and pulls at him with every torture. What reptiles crawl over his creeping limbs! What fiends stand by his midnight pillow! What groans tear his ear! What horrors shiver through his soul! Talk of the rack, talk of the Inquisition, talk of the funeral pyre, talk of the crushing Juggernaut—he feels them all at once.

I suppose, when an inebriate wakes up in the lost world, he will feel an infinite thirst clawing on him. Now, down in the world, although he may have

been very poor, he could beg or he could steal five
cents with which to get that which would slake his
thirst for a little while; but in eternity where is the
rum to come from? Dives could not get one drop
of water. From what chalice of fire will the hot
lips of the drunkard drain his draught? No one to
brew it. No one to mix it. No one to pour it.
No one to fetch it. Millions of worlds then for the
dregs which the young man just now flung on the
sawdusted floor of the restaurant. Millions of worlds
now for the rind thrown out from the punch-bowl
of an earthly banquet. Dives cried for water. The
inebriate cries for rum. Oh, the deep, exhausting,
exasperating, everlasting thirst of the drunkard in
hell! Why, if a fiend came up to earth for some
infernal work in a grog-shop and should go back
taking on its wing just one drop of that for which
the inebriate in the lost world longs, what excitement would it make there! Put that one drop from
off the fiend's wing on the tip of the tongue of the
destroyed inebriate; let the liquid brightness just
touch it; let the drop be very small, if it only have
in it the smack of alcoholic drink; let that drop
just touch the lost inebriate in the lost world, and
he would spring to his feet and cry, "That is rum,
aha! That is rum!" And it would wake up the
echoes of the damned: "Give me rum! Give me
rum! Give me rum!" In the future world I do
not believe that it will be the absence of God that
will make the drunkard's sorrow. I do not believe
that it will be the absence of light. I do not believe

that it will be the absence of holiness. I think it
will be the absence of rum. Oh, "look not upon
the wine when it is red, when it moveth itself aright
in the cup, for at the last it biteth like a serpent,
and it stingeth like an adder."

T. De Witt Talmage, D. D.

THE LIQUOR TRAFFIC ANTAGONISTIC TO AMERICAN LIBERTY.

SOME there are who urge that "the liquor traffic
is an old institution; that the State is composed
of people who have come from different countries
and different nationalities; that the German having
come from his Fatherland has the right to bring
here its customs; that the Irishman coming from
the Evergreen Isle has the right to bring the customs of that country here."

The political customs of this country are the
legitimate children of the social customs and life of
the founders of the Government, of the men who
made our liberties and our institutions possible.

If I ever get indignant in my life, it is when I
hear men born in other countries, together with
dirty, dough-faced American demagogues, sneering
at the Pilgrims, and ridiculing Puritanical morals
and ideas; and I most earnestly protest, in free
America, against the beer smut-mill being turned
on the men who planted our liberties, and suffered
and died to perpetuate them. A few American

sneaks, in order to catch the beer vote, enter the
cemetery where America's noblest dead are buried,
desecrate the graves, and attempt to defile the memory of those who built the Government and established the liberties under which these ghouls live.
Who were these Pilgrims who are now made a by-
word and jest by the beer-guzzlers of this country?
What did they come to America for? What kind of
a country did they find? Britain's poetess answers:

" The breaking waves dashed high
 On a stern and rock-bound coast,
And the woods against a stormy sky
 Their giant branches tossed;
And the heavy night hung dark
 The hills and waters o'er,
When a band of exiles moored their bark
 On the wild New England shore.

Not as the conqueror comes,
 They, the true-hearted, came;
Not with the roll of stirring drums,
 And the trump that sings of fame:
Not as the flying come,
 In silence and in fear;—
They shook the depths of the desert gloom
 With their hymns of lofty cheer.

Amidst the storm they sang,
 And the stars heard, and the sea;
And the sounding aisles of the dim woods rang
 To the anthems of the free.
The ocean eagle soared
 From his nest by the white wave's foam,
And the rocking pines of the forest roared—
 This was their welcome home.

There were men with hoary hair
　Amidst that Pilgrim band:
Why had they come to wither there,
　Away from their childhood's land?
There was woman's fearless eye,
　Lit by her deep love's truth;
There was manhood's brow serenely high,
　And the fiery heart of youth.

What sought they thus afar?
　Bright jewels of the mine?
The wealth of seas, the spoils of war?—
　They sought a faith's pure shrine!
Ay, call it holy ground,
　The soil where first they trod:
They have left unstained what there they found—
　Freedom to worship God."

By struggle and toil, through disease and suffering, they developed the land and planted the ideas
of liberty in their descendants.

Did Americans close the doors of the Republic
and say, "We are free; let the world take care of
itself?" No! They welcomed the down-trodden
of all nations. They have been received as brothers, and made members of the family. After all
this, for these refugees from the despotisms of
Europe to attempt to destroy American customs by
traducing American dead is disgraceful.

The idea that because customs have lived in
another country, and have been developed in another
form of government, they must of right be allowed
to continue here, is utterly fallacious.

The idea that this country has no form, no customs, no laws, no institutions, which immigrants are bound to respect; that men have the right to come here and follow any customs, any ideas, any theories, and any practices, is an idea utterly antagonistic to American institutions, and if carried out will ultimately build on the chaos of our liberties the worst despotism that the world ever saw.

The founders of the Republic recognized the fact that the foundation of universal liberty must be universal education. All the institutions that America inherited have been moulded, shaped, and developed. Among these inherited institutions was the accursed drinking-place. The dram-shop is not a child of American customs, liberty, ideas, schools or theories. It was inherited from the despotic governments of Europe. Its results have been the same as in Europe—drunkenness, debauchery, vice, crime, riot, communism.

Compromise has followed compromise, the unrestrained sale, license, high license, civil damage, local option; and I wish to assert in the light of history that all these compromises have been failures to just the extent that principle has been sacrificed; and successes just to the extent that right has been recognized, and prohibitory features incorporated into their text. Thus this institution has been tested and found unworthy of a place in a free republic. It is an enemy of American liberties, and must be destroyed.

JOHN B. FINCH.

THE GREAT SCOURGE.

HOWEVER viewed, and wherever found, intemperance, in its beginning, its progress, and its end, is everywhere marked by desolation and woe. Alcohol, both in name and in truth, is the poison of our species. Chemical analysis and physiological experiment have established beyond controversy that alcohol, received into the stomach, remains unchanged—unassimilated—and, as such, travels with the blood, through the various arteries, veins, and organs of the system, not as blood nor as its fit companion, but as a murderous associate, a treacherous highwayman, charged with poison and commissioned to destroy.

In its journey round it feeds upon the liver, corrodes the lungs, burns the stomach, ruins the appetite, impairs digestion, discolors and vitiates the blood, defiles the breath, crimsons the nose, parches the lips, blisters the tongue, scalds the throat, husks the voice, bloats the face, dims the eye, wastes the muscles, palsies the limbs, deranges the nerves, and consumes the heart; and, as though its warrant was not yet fully executed, a detached portion of it aims at the head, breaks through its delicate vessels, crowds out reason, and takes up its poisonous, sacrilegious residence on the brain, and fears not to profane Divinity's earthly temple.

But even now its baneful work is hardly begun. Having thus undermined the health, and prepared

the system for the ravages of disease, it strikes at
the moral and intellectual powers of man. It en-
feebles the understanding, impairs the judgment,
effaces the memory, extinguishes sensibility, pollutes the imagination, depraves the taste, stupefies
conscience, annihilates honor, prostrates self-respect,
debases the social affections, sours the disposition,
inflames the wicked passions, dethrones the reason,
and contaminates the heart, and thus quenches
rational life and blots out the moral image of
Deity's handiwork. Why, therefore, must not the
intemperate man become a human fiend? Who is
safe where he is?

And yet its march of ruin is onward still! It
reaches abroad to others, invades the family and
social circle, and spreads woe and sorrow all around.
It cuts down youth in its vigor, manhood in its
strength, and age in its weakness. It breaks the
father's heart, bereaves the doting mother, extinguishes natural affection, erases conjugal love, blots
out filial attachment, blights parental hope, and
brings down mourning age in sorrow to the grave.
It produces weakness, not strength; sickness, not
health; death, not life. It makes wives widows,
children orphans, fathers fiends, and all of them
paupers and beggars. It covers the land with idleness, poverty, disease and crime. It fills your jails,
supplies your almshouses, and demands your asylums. It engenders controversies, fosters quarrels,
and cherishes riots. It contemns law, spurns order,
and loves mobs. It is the life-blood of the gam-

bler, the aliment of the counterfeiter, the prop of the highwayman, and the support of the midnight incendiary.

It countenances the liar, respects the thief, and esteems the blasphemer. It violates obligation, reverences fraud and honors infamy: it defames benevolence, hates love, accuses virtue, and slanders innocence.

It suborns witnesses, nurses perjury, defiles the jury-box, and stains the judicial ermine. It bribes votes, disqualifies voters, corrupts elections, pollutes our institutions, and endangers our government. It degrades the citizen, debases the legislator, dishonors the statesman, and disarms the patriot. It brings shame, not honor; terror, not safety; despair, not hope; misery, not happiness. It poisons felicity, kills peace, ruins morals, blights confidence, slays reputation, and wipes out national honor; then curses the world and laughs at its ruins.

THE NEW DECLARATION OF INDEPENDENCE.

A HEAVIER yoke than that the British king placed upon the neck of our Revolutionary fathers is upon us and our children. A bondage more abject than that which lifted its destroying hand against the Union a score and more of years ago is forging its fetters for the enslavement of the Republic. By a long train of abuses and usurpations King Alcohol, through the liquor traffic in this goodly land, openly declares his ability to reduce us to his despotic rule by his control of the dominant political organizations of the country.

The Republic must triumph over rum, or rum will triumph over the Republic. "All history teaches this ; observation and reason confirm it."

In most of our cities the drinking-saloon is the central power around which politics revolve, and which dictates candidates and party politics. Even in our national elections it sometimes exercises a. controlling influence and decides presidential contests.

This monster, sitting supreme in the politics of this country, has enacted laws authorizing him to open in all our towns and cities slaughter-houses of men, women and children and of all virtue.

He has enacted laws permitting him to transform men into beasts.

He has despoiled labor, burdened property with excessive taxation, impoverished whole communities, hindered education, corrupted morals, fostered crimes, aided all classes of vice and wrong, and plunged his unhappy victims into shame and degradation.

He sits supreme in the National Congress and makes laws in the country's capital.

He governs courts of justice, and makes ministers of the law and legislatures his lackeys.

He silences the preacher in his pulpit and muzzles the editor at his desk.

The time would fail me to tell the thousandth part of the evils, multiplying and destructive, that flow out of the infamous liquor traffic. Oh, for an uprising of righteous indignation, for an aroused American conscience, for patriotic devotion to home and country like that which gave inspiration and faith to Jonas Parker and his neighbors when they reddened the village green of Lexington with their blood on that glorious morning a century and more ago, when the old Revolution burst into magnificent blossoms as the shot was fired that echoed round the world; for an enlightened public opinion, the mightiest advocate of any question; for the combined forces of Christian home, Christian Church and Christian commonwealth in battle array against the traffic in theft and murder, until it shall be thundered from every political Sinai, national and State: "Thou shalt not, and there shall be no legalized saloon where floats the starry flag of the free." Not until then will the infamous business cease; not until then will we be delivered from its Satanic sorceries. Temporizing policies are a failure. Under all systems of license-regulation or tax, the work of ruin and death goes on. Myriads of homes are poisoned, the prosperity of the nation is undermined, the strength of our race wasted, millions are hurried to early and dishonored graves, and a lurid shadow is cast upon the life beyond. The prohibition of the liquor traffic is the demand of the people, and politicians and statesmen who fail to heed it are treasuring up wrath against the day of wrath. Prohibition is in the air. The nation's heart is beginning to throb to its music. Its coming is whispered on every breeze. The rising tide breaks all along the shore, and each succeeding white-fringed billow washes further up the strand.

> "'Tis weary watching wave on wave,
>   And yet the tide heaves onward;
> We build, like corals, grave on grave,
>   But pave a pathway sunward.
> We are beaten back in many a fray,
>   But newer strength we borrow;
> And where the vanguard rests to-day
>   The rear shall camp to-morrow."

Nothing can resist the onward march of a genuine reform. Every such movement enters into and becomes a part of the Messianic purpose to set judgment in the earth. Agitation on this question is the duty of the hour. Let it go on from press, platform and pulpit, in the prayer-meetings and at the ballot-box. until every patriot who loves his country, every Christian who loves his God, every philanthropist who loves his race, every father who loves his child, every son of the Republic will, a marshaled host, uplift the Constitution as a banner of reform, and under its folds march to the ballot-boxes of the land, and under an avalanche of freemen's ballots bury beyond resurrection the American saloon. Then shall our whole Union become the citadel of sobriety, the national name be purged of this great shame, and our glorious banner,

"Whose hues are all of heaven—
Its red the sunset's dye,
The whiteness of the moon-lit cloud,
The blue of morning sky,"

shall be the flag of hope, for all mankind **as it floats**
over our sober, free and happy people.

"O'er the high and o'er the lowly
Floats that banner bright and holy,
In the rays of freedom's sun.
In our nation's heart imbedded,
O'er our Union newly wedded,
One in all and all in one."

GEN. CLINTON B. FISK.

SHALL AMERICA BE RULED FOREVER BY THE LIQUOR POWER?

THERE is a class of men rebellious to all law,
glorying in their rebellion, defying the people
to curb their power—the saloon-keepers. And this
shameless rebellion against law is in order to flood
the land more freely with alcohol, to make drunkards, ruin families, fill jails and poorhouses. The
organ of the liquor dealers pointedly asked the other
day why temperance speakers attack men who are
doing business just as others in the grocery or the
clothing business. The reasons are very plain. No
other business entails woe and sin as the liquor trade,
and no other business is lawless in its methods, and
defiant before the country, as the liquor traffic. **And**

to secure impunity in their lawlessness and to prevent the enactment of new laws, and a wish on the part of the country to enforce any, the saloon-keepers and their leaders are at work to control the politics of the Republic. The charge needs no proof; but the people need to be awakened to the meaning of the fact.

It is not denied that men, whatever their fitness for office, who are not acceptable to the saloon-keepers cannot be elected. The saloon-keepers are interested in the caucus, and from the day of nomination to that of election they have an eye single to business. Ambitious candidates must propitiate the gods either by sworn promise of yeoman service or by limitless orders to treat the " boys." Men in office fear them; their ire is an omen of future political obscurity.

The traffic can . afford to threaten. It wields great power. The traffic is organized; its officers reach upward in the commercial world, and throw around significant nods in banks, stores, and newspaper offices. It is generous in the distribution of coin. There is a great deal at stake, and a present judicious investment will secure large future dividends. The liquor lobby at Albany admitted before a legislative committee that they had expended about $100,000 to influence legislation. State and national parties quail before the traffic. How often sails are trimmed and planks squared in anticipation of the liquor squall! And when the charts of a convention bear tracings of restrictive legislation, the candidates of the convention tremble for their safety unless their strong principles give them courage and law-loving citizens come to their aid. Have you observed how in the very halls of the National Congress, amid incomprehensible amendments and counter-amendments to the revenue laws, one idea is plainly discernible—alcohol's friends mean that they shall be reckoned with?

The cities, very naturally, suffer most from the political manœuvres of the liquor traffic. The liquor men claim for themselves a prescriptive right to seats in a municipal council: other city offices they concede to their friends. It is manifest, though a lamentable fact, that their influence in the cities of America makes void of effect restrictive liquor legislation and establishes the violation of law by the traffic as the normal condition of affairs. Owing to it the government of our large cities has become the problem of the country. Statesmen are alarmed. The terrible conclusion is forcing itself upon thoughtful minds that in cities universal suffrage, the corner-stone of democracy of our peculiar American political institutions, is a failure. It is not the people, it is the populace that rule. And such a populace! Low-minded, rough in manners, uncouth in gait, confirmed in idleness and bent on crime, the terror of well-behaved citizens—such as they must be, brutalized by alcohol.

All this means that we turn the power of government into agencies to foment intemperance—for, to sustain and develop the liquor traffic in its present methods is plainly to foment intemperance. It means that we permit and authorize the exploitation of a vile and tiger-like appetite in the interest of the cupidity and the political power of liquor men. It means that we set the seal of the republic recognizing and approving, upon intemperance and the making of intemperance.

It means, to our national disgrace, that America is ruled by the liquor power. It means that Americans have not the will nor the ability to enforce law, that lawlessness abides with us, that our legislation is mere verbiage. It is difficult to explain the popular indifference to intemperance and the methods of the liquor traffic. It is chiefly, no doubt, due to our ignorance of the actual condition of things.

This indifference is the misfortune. Barren discussions as to the proper methods in dealing with the evil would soon cease were we in earnest in seeking a method. We know not what to do, because we desire to do nothing, and but little if anything will ever be done until the people of America, thoroughly conscious of their danger and of their duty, shall in their indignation and their might declare in thunder tones that the rum-power must cease.

ARCHBISHOP IRELAND.

TRUE VICTORY.

HE stood with a foot on the threshold
   And a cloud on his boyish face,
While his city comrade urged him
   To enter the gorgeous place.

"There's nothing to fear, old fellow!
   It isn't a lion's den.
Here waits you a royal welcome
   From lips of the bravest.men."

'Twas the old, old voice of the tempter
   That sought in the old, old way,
To lure with a lying promise
   The innocent feet astray.

"You'd think it was Blue Beard's closet,
   To see how you stare and shrink!
I tell you there's naught to harm you,—
   It's only a game and a drink!"

He heard the words with a shudder,—
   "It's only a game and a drink!"
And his lips made bold to answer:
   "But what would my mother think?"

The name that his heart held dearest
   Had started a secret spring,
And forth from the wily tempter
   He fled like a hunted thing.

Away! till the glare of the city
   And its gilded halls of sin
Are shut from his sense and vision
   The shadows of night within.

Away! till his feet have bounded
   O'er fields where his childhood trod;
Away! in the name of virtue
   And the strength of his mother's God!"

What though he was branded "coward!"
   In the blazoned halls of vice,
And banned by his baffled tempter,
   Who sullenly tossed the dice.

On the page where the angel keepeth
   The record of deeds well done,
That night was the story written
   Of a glorious battle won.

And he stood by his home in the starlight,
   All guiltless of sword and shield,
A braver and nobler victor
   Than the hero of bloodiest field!

M. A. MAITLAND.

OUR REGIMENTS OF REFORM.

THE present attitude of the temperance cause is a bewilderment in many minds. "What next?" is the question being asked with moist eye and trembling voice. What we want now is to mass all our troops of all shades of belief. I look off in many directions, and see the regiments of reform are doing splendid work. Some of them are shooting this way and some are shooting that way, and some are shooting into the air. I put the field-glass to my eye and I look off in one direction, and I see the regiments of the Sons of Temperance, who have already saved enough men to make a good-sized heaven. Good cheer to them! I put the field-glass to my eye and I look off in another direction, and I see the regiments of the Good Templars, who are girdling the earth with their benedictions. They have a pass-word in their association. I know not what it is, but I suggest as the pass-word most appropriate for them the word "Victory." Good cheer to them! I put the field-glass to my eye and I look off in another direction, and I see the regiments of the Rechabites, who since 1835 have been filling the air with sounds of mercy and emancipation and the crash of broken wine-pitchers. Good cheer to them! I put the field-glass to my eye and I look off in another direction, and I see the regiments of brave women. These are the Deborahs who fear not to go out and fight the iron chariots of opposition when even the knees of Barak tremble. Good cheer to them! I put the field-glass to my eye and I look off again, and I see the great regiments of the Prohibitionists, who are doing their chief work in the establishment of laws which shall make the manufacture and sale of intoxicating liquor an impossibility. And God will in the end give them complete success, even though Supreme Courts should revoke all favorable decisions. There is a higher power than human power. No one can doubt the issue if ever there should be placed upon the calendar a case like this: "The Lord God Almighty versus The Supreme Court of the United States." About the result of such a contest there can be no uncertainty.

Mass all the troops, all the regiments of temperance reform, not for a Bridge of Lodi, but for a Waterloo. Why not a Waterloo? We have enough men; we have enough artillery; we have enough courage; we have enough Wellingtons; we have enough Bluchers; we have enough reinforcements; and coming in on our side is the God of Samuel and David and Joshua—him of Megiddo, him of the Valley of Ajalon. The Lord of hosts now strikes His hand upon His thigh until the sword rattles in His buckler, while He declares that no weapon formed against us shall prosper. It has been decreed in high heaven that sin must go down and righteousness must triumph. Do you believe in our final victory? If not, get out! Cross over to the other side. Better is an armed foe than a weak-kneed coadjutor. I suppose that it seemed ridiculous when Moses stretched out his hand over the Red Sea. What power could that have over the waters? But the east wind blew all night; the waters gathered into two adamantine walls on either side; the billows reared as God's hand pulled back upon their crystal bits. Wheel into line, O

Israel! March! march! Pearls crash under the feet. The flying spray springs a rainbow arch over the victors. The shout of hosts mounting the beach answer the shout of hosts mid-sea; until, as the last line of the Israelites has gained the beach, the shields clang and the cymbals clap; and as the waters whelm the pursuing foe, the swift-fingered winds on the white keys of the foam play the grand march of Israel delivered, and the awful dirge of Egyptain overthrow. So we go forth, and stretch out the hand of prayer and Christian effort over the Red Sea of alcoholism and crime. "Aha! aha!" say the deriding world. But wait. The winds of divine help will begin to blow; the way will clear for the great army of Christian philanthropists; the glittering treasures of the world's beneficence will line the path of our feet; and to the other shore we will be greeted with the clash of all heaven's cymbals; while those who resist and deride and pursue us will fall under the sea, and there will be nothing left of them, but here and there, cast high and dry upon the beach, the splintered wheel of a chariot, and thrust out from the surf the breathless nostril of a riderless charger. Mighty God! save us, and save our families, and save the land from the scathing, scalding, blasting, damning influence of strong drink!

T. DE WITT TALMAGE, D. D.

FAILURE.

COME, John, sit down by me; it frets my soul
    To see you walking up and down the room.
The thud of your slow feet is like the fall
Of clods into a grave.   I can not bear
To see that head, that never stooped before,
Bowed on your breast in tearless agony—
It maddens me, for well I know you feel
The deep disgrace of rearing drunken sons
More than the grief of losing.

                Come, sit down,
For all my mother instincts are awake,
And longings fierce, intense and tigerish prove
All mothers—beasts or women—are alike.
I almost hate you for your pride.   Your face
Is rigid and monotonous and drear
As some dry desert.   Is there no remorse
Gnawing your heart-strings?   Does no sorrow thrum
The tight-drawn strings of pain until your heart
Is numb with aching?

                Oh, the glorious strength
Of manhood, that can find no room for grief
For very pride of heart!   Oh, selfish men!
What do you know of woman?   In her two-fold life
The mother learns a deeper mystery
Of pain and pleasure.   In her child she lives,
And suffers, and is happy.   She can feel
The joy and grief-throbs of its little heart

In her responsive breast. The child is but
A little of herself—the good is hers,
And even the very worst her secret heart
Owns for its own and covers with a veil of palliation.
Oh, my wayward boy! my erring lost one!

Yes—I will be calm—
Your voice could always calm me. You can tell
How many years since you have held me thus
Close to your breast, my husband? Does it seem
So long since you were young? To me the past
Is but yesterday. I could believe
It was last week we sat talking thus
With our one boy—your pride, my all in all—
Crowing and tossing up his small, fat hands
In awkward baby grace upon our laps.
Have you forgotten, John, that summer's night
When we were wondering what his life would be
When he grew up? And how you proudly said
That some day Johnny should be President;
But I said I loved best to think him still
A little baby, nestling his small head
Close to my breast, and looking up to mine
With pleading eyes for comfort in his pain.
And then you laughed and told me I would spoil
The boy with petting. Ah, John, who spoiled most?
You, with your noble sternness, sparing not
Your heart nor his to force him to grow up
Straight-trunked and fruitful, like yourself; or I,
Twining my love about him like a vine,
To hide his rugged branches with green leaves?

I know we both were wrong; but you the most,
For you forget that to the little shoot
God whispers how to grow; the husbandman
But loosens the hard soil, pulls out the weeds,
And gives its growth free way.   You tried to raise
An oak from a young thorn—my woman's eyes
Softened its fibres with too many rains.
We could do better, John, if God had pleased
To trust us to bring up another son.
Alas, we have none other; this was all!
This, that refused to walk in the straight road,
Rocky and flowerless, that you made for him;
But jumped the hedges and ran his own wild course
Among the snares and pitfalls; this, that brought
Shame to your head, and sorrow to my heart—
That left our door that stormy winter night
With your grim benediction and my prayers
Following his staggering steps; this, that came home
Only last night with his young limbs all gashed
And crunched by cruel car wheels, was our all—
Our baby boy that, some short years ago,
We tossed and kissed between us.

   O my God!
And shall I never see my boy again?
I can not think of "never."   Shall to-day
Succeed to yesterday, and yesterday
Glide backward to last year; the years grow old,
And each in passing leaves a few grey hairs
And a new grief-mark, till my head is white
And my face seamed and ugly; shall my strength
Ooze out a grain a day, till my light step

Becomes a feeble hobble?   Shall I still
Live on, and on, and on, and die at last
Of utter uselessness, and until death
Still yearn, and yearn, and never see him once?
O God, I can not bear it!

Let me go!
You can not comfort me with Scripture texts,
Nor make me say that it is better so.
I know he brought down shame upon our heads—
I know he was a drunkard, and his
Life one round of vice and crime—but he was mine;
Crime could not make him a thing so low
But he could love his mother, and that love
Was more to me than goodness.   Ah, who knows
How many times he may have longed to come
And lay his head upon her breast again,
And your cold looks prevented—who can tell
What angel guided home his reeling steps
That awful night—who knows what might have been
But for your bitter words that drove him back
To perish in the storm?

Nay, John, come back!
It is a fearful thing to see you weep.
Forgive my cruel words, for I am wild
With longing for my boy.   You are the tower
That shelters me.   I could not bear to have
You other than you are—firm, rocky, strong;
But I am like a foolish mother-bird
Whose nest is empty.   Bear with me awhile
Till I have grown acquainted with my grief,

And learn to call it friend, and weep with it
In quiet hours alone.

      This dreadful hour
Brings us old age. I must give up my dreams,
And you your high ambitions. Once again
We must be lovers, John, and so make smooth
The rocky hill of life, whose steep descent
We must go down together. Kiss me, John.
                        CHARLES QUIET.

NO SURRENDER! NO COMPROMISE!

IT is a fact that ninety-nine per cent. of all the genuine temperance work, in educating the public sentiment, in securing sobriety in the youth of the land, in reforming the intemperate, and in creating sound legislative enactments, that has been done for the past forty years, and that is being done to-day, is the work of the friends of total abstinence:

> "They may laugh at her name,
> They may blazon her shame,
> But there's life in the old tree yet."

Total abstinence and prohibition have carried our cause to the high-water mark of the hour. We will not repudiate them; we will not permit the enemy to suggest new methods, to invent tactics for us, or to clandestinely capture and spike our guns. When the foe proposes compromise, when dealers and drinkers get up a temperance society, keep your mind on the wooden horse of the Greeks, and keep the walls of the city intact. "Beware the Greeks, bearing presents." To entrust the Roman Empire to Catiline's band of traitors is madness! The "Old Guard" of the temperance cause know how to die, but not how to surrender. When the devil joins the church it is a symptom of serious illness. Strategy has supplanted open battle. "Put none but Americans on guard." We have fought too long and hard, and have gained too great vantage-ground, to think of compromise with a scared enemy. We have nothing to gain and everything to lose by an armistice. We have aroused public opinion; we have aroused the Church as never before; we have created a powerful temperance literature; we have been reinforced by the artillery of science; we have won to our side the majesty of law; we have enlisted the prayers and purpose, patience and persistence, of legions of Christian women; we have been cheered by the signal benedictions of God, and compromise or surrender of total abstinence and prohibition would be shameless treason.

No moral question is ever finally settled until settled in harmony with the principles of uncompromising truth and justice and righteousness:

> "For right is right, since God is God,
> And right our cause shall win;
> To doubt would be disloyalty,
> To falter would be sin."

God thunders against all compromise with evil, and foretells certain defeat: "And your covenant with death shall be disannulled, and your agreement with hell shall not stand when the overflowing scourge shall pass through, then shall ye be trodden down by it." The least compromise with evil is moral treason to God. Our only business is to fight evil with relentless purpose. Half-and-half men can not be relied on. Sandy was a jolly Scotchman and great dancer. Converted, he joined the Church and quit dancing. One day on the street the bagpipes came by, playing shrill and loud the Highland Fling. Sandy began to dance wildly with one foot, keeping the other fixed on the sidewalk. "Mon," said a bystander, "are ye lame?" "Nae! nae! but one fut belongs to the church, while the ither is wild as the de'il." We want men to stand square on both feet for total abstinence, and to resist the sorcery of the bagpipes when they play champagne suppers or a bottle of wine at dinner. But didn't Paul advise Timothy to take "a little wine"? Yes. Hear it: "Drink no longer water, but use a little wine for thy stomach's sake and thine often infirmities." Ah! here is the proof that Timothy was a teetotaler, a cold-water man, so radical and abstemious that, amid manifold infirmities, Paul has to plead with him to try it as a medicine. If he had not been a total abstainer, Paul would not have been obliged to urge him to change his habits. Oh! for a generation of cold-water men like Timothy, that nothing short of a revelation from God by an inspired apos-

tle could induce to touch wine even as a medicine!
And there is not a hint that Timothy ever touched
it even then. But didn't Christ make wine at
Cana? Yes. Then may we not drink it? Yes,
when Almighty God makes it for you, by a miracle,
out of water. Therefore, by logic of facts glanced
at, in experience, science, in Scripture, in safety to
the young, in non-complicity with the gigantic evil
in any form, we salute our loyal banner with cheers,
and keep it flying over the citadel of total abstinence,
bearing our brave legend, "No surrender! No compromise!"

REV. J. O. PECK, D. D.

THE DEACON'S SUNDAY-SCHOOL SERMON.

A DEAR old deacon in my State was cursed with a
high license pulpit, but was so loyal to the
church that he took as Gospel all that fell from the
desk. So, when his pastor pushed high license,
he as Superintendent of the Sunday-school said:
"Teach it to the children; as the trees are bent, the
twigs should be inclined." So in his homely way he
turned the sermons into language the children could
understand, and made a talk for high license before
the Sunday-school.

"Dear boys and girls," began the deacon, "you
know it's very naughty to drink beer and whisky.
So, too, it's naughty to sell them without a license,
or with a cheap license. But when the State orders

high license, and the town makes every saloon-keeper pay it, $500 out of what he gets for making drunkards, it isn't naughty any longer to sell beer and whisky, but a real nice, respectable business like selling sugar or hymn books. And your blessed papas don't like to have a fifty dollar saloon close by their store; but with a five hundred dollar one each side they know that all good people will like to visit their store. So, when bad men get drunk and swear and fight and roll into the gutter before the five hundred dollar saloon, your high license papas know that's a blessing, and they must thank God every day that blessings fall so thick about them.

"You see it all clear, don't you, children? If not, you must be patient, and remember your eyes will grow bigger, like pa's, some day. Of course, too, your fine mammas never visit the wife of that fifty dollar rum-seller; but quick as he grows so good and respectable that he pays his town $500 a year as its share of what he gets by making drunkards and drunkards' wives and children, and the old tax-payers pat him on the back, why then, of course, your fine mammas go right off and visit his wife, and find her just lovely, and ask her over to tea; don't they? You know an advance of $450 in license works a great change of heart and manners in the saloon-keeper and all his family; when he pays $50 he's a brute, but when he pays $500 he's a gentleman.

"You keep on seeing it, don't you, children? Maybe, though, you can't see why, if it's awful wicked for a fifty dollar license to fill a man's boots

with snakes and his head with the crazy, and turn
his hands into double fists, and send him home to
knock down his wife and kick his little boy and girl
into the street—if this is dreadful wicked, maybe
you can't quite see why it's all right and respectable
for a five hundred dollar license to do the same
thing. But it'll come clear to you when you grow
up and read the Bible the way lots o' men do now.
Then you'll see that what's all wrong standing alone,
is all right standing on $500.

"Maybe, too, pet lambs, you don't now quite see
how, if it's wrong to drink liquors at any license,
it's right as can be to sell them at any license, coax-
ing men to drink them. But wait till you get big,
and hear men talk who know a pious lot about high
license. Then you'll see that the words in the Lord's
prayer—'Lead us not into temptation'—don't mean
anything now, the world's got to be so smart. And
when the license preachers get up a new version of
the Testament, I suppose they'll leave out all that
nonsense.

"One thing more, sweet ones: Don't forget what
a high license is to poor towns. Why, quite often it
builds a new jail—and fills it. Isn't that real good
of it? So, if any of you die drunkards, or drunkards' wives, it'll be a warm comfort to you to remember that, by living drunk, or with a drunkard,
you've paid to support your town and country,
almost one-tenth of what they've paid to kill you.

"You must remember, too, that it's because intemperance is wrong that high license is right. It's

so much, you see, like Prohibition; for you can easily see that 'a half loaf's better'n no bread,' if 'tis poison.

"Now, good-by, children; and if ever you want to be constable, or go to Congress, and want the taxes collected in a tumbler, don't object to being cursed, only charge high for it."

The Sunday-school scholars laughed and called the deacon crazy, their fathers got to thinking, and the pastor got into a passion, but was afterward converted and became a good man.

JAMES CLEMENT AMBROSE.

HOW TO CUR-TAIL THE LIQUOR TRAFFIC.

IT was in Arcady. The Council of State, made up of patriarchs with gentle eyes and long beards, sat meditating on measures pertaining to the public weal. The door was suddenly thrown open and a lad, breathless, with cheeks flushed and eyes bulging out with excitement, after several vain efforts to articulate, at length succeeded in saying, "Your Honors,—there's a mad dog—rampaging the streets!"

"Mad dog rampaging the streets!"

In a moment all was confusion. The aged counsellors sprang to their feet and stood silent with suppressed excitement. Then as with one impulse they all hastened to the front windows of the Consilium.

"There he is!" cried out one of them presently.

"Where? Where?"

"See him? Yonder by the Cross-roads at the Market!"

"Ah, yes! And, oh, horrors! how he is foaming and raging! Woe to any helpless ones that may chance to come before him."

"See by the Pantheon," cried another; the children are just coming from morning school! They will surely be bitten by this mad beast!"

And bitten they were. One and another of them were torn by his poisonous fangs.

"Oh, this is horrible!" cried one of the venerable men at the window.

"What shall be done about it?"

"Aye, that's the practical question, what shall be done about it?"

"Let us consult the Legalia Convella!"

The Legalia Convella were the Books of Law, the accumulated wisdom of many ages. The sages sat solemnly bending over the books. Day after day they had turned over the parchment leaves with no mentionable results. Meanwhile the original mad dog had bitten many others, and there were now scores and hundreds of raging curs, foaming at the lips, hiding at every corner and ready to spring forth upon the passers-by.

The people mourned. There was lamentation in almost every house. People were bitten and limped or were carried to their homes, where, after weeks of lingering pain, they died in awful spasms. Still the deliberations went on at the Consilium. The aged functionaries were unwilling to do anything without the authority of law, and as yet they had been able to find nothing. At length, as they were poring over the Convella, a gleam of sudden joy lighted the face of one of them and he cried, "I have it; here it is!"

They looked up eagerly, then all bending over the book read as follows:

"Be it ordained : That in case any beast shall so rage and rave as to endanger the public safety, his tail shall forthwith be cut off."

"His tail cut off!"

"What good will that do? A dog don't bite with his tail."

"No, but he isn't apt to bite so hard if his tail is cut off."

"We don't believe it! We don't believe it!" cried many voices!

"Well, anyway, if we abbreviate the tails of these dogs, we shall be better able to regulate their doings."

"Why so?"

"Because there won't be so much of the dogs to regulate."

"And besides we shall lend a respectable air to the whole business in this way."

"How?"

"Why, after cutting off their tails, it will be evident that the law has nothing more against them. This will make rabid dogs respectable, and biting a legitimate business."

"Yes, and it will increase our revenues."

"How do you make that out?"

"Why, we can levy on the people a tax of one dollar for every tail cut off."

"Enough of this nonsense. What we want to do is to get rid of this whole infernal business. A dog with his tail cut off is just as hard to regulate as a dog with a tail a yard long. And it is no economy to increase the public revenues by a drain on the people's purses. Neither do you gain anything by making mad dogs respectable and a bad business legitimate. What we want to do is simply and solely to stop this rabid biting in the streets." (It was a prohibitionist who spoke—a fanatic.)

Then there was silence for a long while. The Regulators could find nothing to say.

"I have it, I have it!" at length cried one.

"Where?"

Then he read:

"Be it ordained: That in case any beast shall so rage and rave as to endanger the public safety, his tail shall forthwith be cut off."

"Why, that's precisely what we had before."

"Yes, but it is enough; it will suppress the evil; no need of our exceeding the law."

"How do you make that out?"

"Why, don't you see, the law doesn't say where the dog's tail shall be cut off!"

"Well?"

"Suppose we cut it off just back of his ears."

This was approved.

The thing was done.

The dogs' tails were cut off just back of their ears. That was curtailing the business with a vengeance.

It was prohibition. There was no regulation about it.

But this curtailing proved most effective. The mad-dog business was done with forever.

Everybody said, "Why didn't we think of it before?"

And when the old counsellor died who had conceived the happy thought, they built a monument over him bearing this inscription:

TO THE MEMORY OF TEETOTALIS PROHIBITUS,

Who originated the maxim. "The proper place to curtail a bad business is just back of its ears."

I'LL TAKE WHAT FATHER TAKES.

T'was in the flow'ry month of June,
    The sun was in the west,
When a merry, blithesome company
    Met at a public feast.

Around the room rich banners spread,
    And garlands fresh and gay;
Friend greeted friend right joyously
    Upon that festal day.

The board was filled with choicest fare;
    The guests sat down to dine;
Some called for "bitters" some for "stout,"
    And some for rosy wine.

Among this joyful company
  A modest youth appeared.
Scarce sixteen summers had he seen:
  No specious snare he feared.

An empty glass before the youth
  Soon drew the waiter near.
"What will you take, sir," he inquired—
  "Stout, bitter, mild, or clear?

"We've rich supplies of foreign port,
  We've first-class wine and cakes."
The youth, with guileless look, replied:
  "I'll take what father takes."

Swift as an arrow went the words
  Into his father's ears,
And soon a conflict deep and strong
  Awoke terrific fears.

The father looked upon his son,
  Then gazed upon the wine;
O God! he thought, were he to taste,
  Who could the end divine?

Have I not seen the strongest fall,
  The fairest led astray?
And shall I on my only son
  Bestow a curse this day?

No; Heaven forbid! "Here, waiter, bring
  Bright water unto me.
My son will take what father takes—
  My drink shall water be."

W. Hoyle.

DRINK'S DOINGS.

GRIM war has slain its millions,
  Plague filled its myriad graves,
And thousands have gone down to deaths
  Amid the ocean waves.

The mountain-rending earthquake
  Hath many, many slain,
And fire and famine seized their prey
  In city, town, and plain.

But drink, the fell destroyer,
  Hath slaughtered more by far
Than earthquake, famine, fire, or sea,
  Or pestilence or war.

WHO'LL BE THE DRUNKARDS THEN.

MY friends and brethren, Templars true,
  Some questions I would ask.
Who'll occupy the place you fill,
Who'll fight the demon of the still,
  When you have passed away?
Our boys, say you, will soon be men,
And they will fight the demon then.
They'll occupy the place we fill,
And work and pray and labor till
  There dawns a brighter day.

Who, think you, then will keep saloons,
   Gin-palaces, and dives?
Who'll brew and mash, distil and sell?
I think that may be I can tell
   Who'll be the liquor-men:
The boys Good Templars cannot reach,
The little folks we fail to teach;
The bright-eyed boys I've seen in schools,
Who're taught that temperance men are fools.
   They'll be the liquor-men.

Who'll fill the jails in after-years,
   By alcohol enslaved?
Who'll spend their earnings for strong drink?
Just pause awhile now, brother; think!
   Who'll be the drunkards then?
The boys who wander up and down,
The little smokers you have met—
The boys with pipe or cigarette—
   Will be the drunkards then.

Now, then, should we just let things run,
   As we are apt to do?
Or should we start with willing feet
To gather in from lane or street
   These boys of eight and ten?
For every one we train aright
May live to be a man of might,
May keep his pledge, and then, you see,
One thing is certain—that is, he
   Won't be a drunkard then.
                THOS. R. THOMPSON.

Sunday School and Church

⊷ ENTERTAINMENTS. ⊷

HANDSOMELY ENGRAVED COVER.

Paper Binding, 30 cts.   **Cloth, 50 cts.**

IT is seldom so many requests have been made for a book as have come to us for a work of this character.

The want has not only been widespread but of long duration as well. An earlier issue would have been made had the right kind of material offered or the services of a suitable editor been secured. We have satisfied ourselves in both these respects, and are confident our judgment will be confirmed by every person using the book.

While each article is new and original, none have been inserted without first being critically examined, not only for their attractiveness and literary merit, but also for their particular adaptability to some of the various phases of Sunday School and Church Entertainments.

The articles are largely in the nature of Dialogues, Tableaux, Recitations, Concert Pieces, Motion Songs, and Short Dramas, all based upon or illustrating some biblical truths. In several instances familiar bible stories are dramatized with simplicity and yet with power.

Special care has been taken to make provision for such occasions as Christmas, New Year's, Easter, and Thanksgiving, so that no time or season is without a subject.

Sold by all Booksellers and Newsdealers, or mailed upon receipt of price.

THE PENN PUBLISHING COMPANY

1020 Arch Street

Philadelphia

Sunday ✧ School ✧ Selections

By JOHN H. BECHTEL

Engraved Cover. 200 Pages

Paper Binding, 30 cents; Cloth, 50 cents

THIS book is much broader in scope than its title implies. The pastor will find much in it to point a moral or adorn a sermon; the superintendent to illustrate and enforce the Sunday School Lesson; the teacher to illumine his teaching; and the general reader to refresh his soul.

With about one hundred and fifty selections of unusual merit, something will be found adapted to every period of life and to every occasion and condition where a choice reading or recitation may be wanted. The Church Social, the Sunday School Concert, Teachers' Gatherings, Meetings of Christian Endeavor Societies, Young Men's Christian Associations, Temperance Unions, Anniversary occasions, and every assemblage of a religious or spiritual character has been provided for.

In point of newness and freshness few compilations compare with this. The selections are drawn from many sources, the result of years of patient gathering. But few of them have appeared before in book form, and nothing hackneyed has been admitted.

The lofty spiritual ideals presented by many of the authors and the rich literary dress in which their thoughts are clad will command for this volume a place high above that occupied by most books of its class.

THE PENN PUBLISHING COMPANY

1020 Arch Street

Philadelphia